D1504481

# Raw

# Justice

# ALSO AVAILABLE BY JK ELLEM

## Stand Alone Novels
*Mill Point Road*
*All Other Sins*

## The Killing Seasons
*Book 1 A Winter's Kill*
*Book 2 A Spring Kill – coming soon*

## No Justice Series
*Book 1 No Justice*
*Book 2 Cold Justice*
*Book 3 American Justice*
*Book 4 Hidden Justice*
*Book 5 Raw Justice*

## Deadly Touch Series
*Fast Read Deadly Touch*

## Octagon Trilogy (DystopianThriller Series)
*Prequel Soldiers Field*
*Book 1 Octagon*
*Book 2 Infernum*
*Book 3 Sky of Thorns – coming soon*

# Raw

# Justice

## by JK Ellem

Copyright © by 28th Street Multimedia Group 2020

# Acknowledgment

A special thanks to Linda H. Bergeron, Douglas W. Jantz and Renee Arthur for your continued support, assistance and constructive feedback, it is extremely appreciated.

To my readers, who inspire me every day, an even bigger thanks – happy reading!

# Chapter 1

Sadness, eternal and unrelenting, was buried there. She could feel it, knew it with absolute certainty.

To her right—from where Sam Rubino stood—a blur of fur threaded its way through trees and knee-high scrub, cutting and weaving, mist swirling in its wake, never faltering as it followed an invisible stream of dead hair follicles, brittle bones, and decaying skin cells. Eighty pounds of grim, silent determination fashioned into muscle, sinew, and canine teeth that could just as easily rip your throat out as it could delicately separate a single molecule of scent from a billion others.

A ghost looking for a ghost.

Sam stood perfectly still, swamp and forest all around her, and continued to watch the blur of fur as it worked its magic, a sight that even now, never ceased to amaze her. Forget about wizards and witches, of wands and broomsticks, of spells and curses. Real magic was unfolding right before her very eyes, as it had done hundreds of times before. Magic that science still couldn't explain as three hundred million olfactory receptors— far more than any human had—went to work all at once, detecting, analyzing, separating, discarding before moving on.

At her back, Sam could feel impatient, doubtful eyes on her, mixed together with too much testosterone. A hundred yards behind her, a line of deputies stood in front of their SUVs in the predawn gloom, watching with cynical thoughts. Sam cut a lonely, solitary figure in the middle of the clearing, the sky dull and bleak, like how she felt right now.

1

The blur of fur suddenly pivoted back on itself, as though an invisible leash had been jerked tight around its neck, making the animal suddenly switch direction.

The scent was stronger now.

He was searching for her, a girl not quite the woman she was destined to become. Someone had seen to that. In another life the dog would have allowed the girl to touch him, to let her tentative, warm fingers reach out and feel the softness of his coat, the menagerie of muted blacks and charcoal grays. She would have marveled at his restrained menace and the beating power in his chest.

Two junior deputies, arms folded with indifference, hips resting on the warm hood of a Madison County sheriff's SUV, exchanged glances. "You know she named her dog, Ghost. Weird isn't it?" the tall one remarked.

The other shrugged. "Kind of appropriate, don't you think?"

The tall one frowned. "How so?"

"A ghost—searching for the ghost of another. No better person to find the dead."

The tall deputy rolled his eyes. This was too profound for 6:00 a.m., especially in some cold, damp, swampy forest in the middle of nowhere.

Sam continued to watch as the blur of fur stopped momentarily, adjusted its internal compass, then bounded off again to where its senses were drawn the most.

The sadness closer now, imminent.

Sam could feel it in the sucking mud under the soles of her boots. Feel it in the damp tendrils of mist that lingered around her ankles. She couldn't smell it—yet. But Ghost could, and that was good enough for her.

Ghost suddenly stopped, nose to ground, vacuuming the rug

of cold mud, brittle leaves, and forest debris. He then settled back on his haunches, looked back to where Sam was standing, his head just above the weeds and rushes, his face forlorn. Their eyes met, and he called to her, a deep, chesty bellow that echoed in the heavy silence.

*Found.*

Then commotion behind her. Arms unfolded, postures straightened, feet shuffled and stomped in the cold, earthy quagmire. Doubt gave way to disbelief. Smirks reformed into smiles. Disrespect became mutual admiration. This young civilian woman, a volunteer, and her dog had done what better-resourced and better-equipped police K-9 units hadn't.

Looking at Ghost, Sam gave a faint smile that no one else could see, and her love for the dog went up a notch, if that was at all possible, while her heart felt a little heavier. She wasn't alone anymore. Someone was there, with her, next to where Ghost now sat obediently.

Sam guessed it was Molly Cotter, the younger of the two sisters. It made sense to her anyway; use the younger sister to control the older; make the older more malleable to do his bidding, to perhaps tie the younger girl first; use her to tell lies to stop the other's incessant crying and sobbing.

Then when it was time, when all hope turned to hopelessness, and the end came into view, kill the younger one first.

Pairs being abducted were unusual—unusually cruel, that is, for the family and everyone involved. It left a hole twice as wide and infinitely as deep in the hearts and minds of those now condemned to a lifetime of suffering with their loss—losses. Two gone, ripped away.

At least by the end of today, Sam would give the family some closure. It was all she could do, partially close the wound that never stopped bleeding and would never quite heal over.

Sensing restlessness behind her, Sam held up her hand, halting any thoughts of anyone coming forward, encroaching on her territory, until she was done. Preservation of the scene was critical to her, and she needed confirmation first on what she knew in her heart when she and Ghost had arrived on scene an hour ago. Slipping on gloves, Sam edged forward, delicate, careful steps. Leaves and twigs crinkled underfoot, and the mud hissed and squelched as she went, making a line toward where Ghost sat, proud and now excited, a smile on his face as only a dog owner could recognize.

Sam arrived and glanced down. The earth was split, cut like skin, giving her up, pushing out what didn't belong there under the surface. A tangle of limbs, blotches of red, and purples over bleached flesh, colors so vibrant, so out of place against the muted woodland pattern. Sam gave a sigh as she squatted down and regarded the orifice in the earth. She began comparing the photos she had committed to memory from the case file to what she was now looking at.

It was Molly Cotter, aged twelve. Sister to Mary-Jane Cotter, aged fifteen. Daughter of Janet and Michael Cotter, whose ages didn't matter. All that mattered was finding who had done this.

Why did it always have to be like this? Why was it that more often than not, the first time Sam met someone was when they were already dead?

It hardly seemed fair.

The case file back at the motel contained a number of photos of the sisters, but Sam, for reasons she couldn't explain, was drawn to the photos of Molly. Molly with her tiny hands wrapped vehemently around the handle bars of her birthday present, all tassels and bells. Molly, all bright smiles and white teeth, golden skin from countless summers spent at the lake. Molly, smiling at the camera in her Grade 7 form photo, glitter ribbons in her hair. All of these images were fading to the reality of what Sam's eyes now saw.

Both sisters had vanished two months ago, taken from their beds. Now one had been found, the other wouldn't be too far away, Sam imagined. She stood and gestured toward the sheriff and her contingent of deputies.

As they descended around the shallow grave, Sam retreated to the periphery as was always the case. She had done her job and she was pushed aside. A nod here, a pat on her back there. But her role was over, for the time being. She found the pieces of a puzzle for others to solve.

Ghost dutifully followed Sam back to a safe distance, and as she stood watching proceedings, she felt the cold wetness of his nose prod her fingers. Without looking down, her hand touched his muzzle and stroked it. Then she took a small rubber chew toy from her pocket and gave it to him before uttering, "Good boy."

An hour later they found the naked body of Mary-Jane Cotter nearby. And just like her younger sister, the animals and the elements hadn't been kind to her.

# Chapter 2

They had known each other since they were both thirteen years old, were neighbors living in the town of Essen, in the Rhineland, northwestern Germany.

Now, five years later, they were engaged.

Martin Fassen was keen to be married, start a family with Karla, despite his parents telling him he was too young, not to flit away the chance he had to study engineering, as his father had, at LMU Munich. Maybe that was why he had defied them, ignored their protests, and fled with Karla to America on tourist visas.

They both loved the outdoors, could have backpacked through their own homeland. But it was the pull of America that had appealed to them both, the land of opportunity where anything was possible, despite the fact that the drinking age was twenty-one, five years more than in Germany.

Karla was a free spirit, had no real plans for the future—including starting a family. However, she agreed to Martin's proposal and saw being engaged as a "trial run" to marriage, something you could drag on without any real legal commitment and back out of at any moment.

And children? The thought of being up to her unshaven armpits in dirty diapers and baby vomit was about as appealing as giving up parties, drugs, getting drunk, and having carefree sex, which they had been indulging in with each other since they had both turned sixteen. These thoughts she kept to herself.

"I need to pee," Karla protested, the weight of Martin crushing down on her.

"What? Now?"

Karla pushed Martin off. "I can't hold on," she said, sitting up inside the tent and pulling on just a gray sweatshirt over her nakedness. She threw Martin a sly smile. "Or I could just piss on you while you're inside me. Something kinky for a change."

"Gross!" Martin proclaimed, rolling onto his back on the air mattress, his manhood—that Karla had just managed to resuscitate into semi-hardness during the last ten minutes—now wilting like a stalk of dehydrated celery. "It will stink up the tent." He watched with fascination as Karla slipped on her sneakers and stretched the baggy sweatshirt over her knees. No pants and definitely no panties, she pivoted around on her knees and almost thrust her buttocks into Martin's face. Having a two-person tent did have its advantages, he thought, watching with sudden interest the pink cleft between Karla's perfectly round and firm ass, which he so desperately wanted to bury his face into.

"Hurry back," Martin moaned, feeling his celery stalk come vaguely alive again as he watched Karla unzip the tent and scuttle out on all fours into the fading light.

Suddenly Karla stuck her head back inside the tent, her eyes dropping to Martin's groin. "Play with it until I get back. You need the practice." She gave a playful smile before disappearing outside again.

Martin lay back, stared up at the nylon ceiling of the tent, and gave a sigh of exasperation. Ever since they had first slept together, he knew he would never be able to keep up with Karla's ravenous libido, let alone fully satisfy her. That had certainly been the attraction of her since their first date, when she took him home and threw him on her parent's bed while they were out at the opera. What young-blooded male wouldn't want a woman who was sexually more voracious than them? At times he felt like the luckiest man in the world, to have a girlfriend—fiancée—who wore him out sexually. Then there were times when he felt worried, almost fearful she would leave him, search out another man, an alpha male who could satisfy her insatiable appetite.

Martin gave another sigh, closed his eyes, and went back to what Karla had instructed.

It wasn't so much a latrine as it was just a shallow, damp hole in the ground, which Martin had dug with a camping shovel behind a large tree with a toilet roll sticking through a low branch he had trimmed down. Karla had insisted the makeshift toilet be at least a hundred yards from where they had pitched the tent the day before. As she trudged through the woods, the light fading with every step she took, she was now regretting that insistence.

Karla hurried, not wanting to find her way back in the dark. Up ahead she could see the tree, the urge to pee swiftly increasing at the sight.

Then she stopped, cocked her head, and looked around, certain she had heard a sound, somewhere in the woods, to her left. But all she could see was a wall of trees and foliage of the silent woods around her.

Maybe nothing, just her imagination.

Unable to hold on any longer, Karla set off again, made it to the tree just in time, squatted over the hole in the ground, and let out a steamy gush. It was the best feeling in the world.

While she waited, Karla looked around at the forest.

Then she heard another sound, this time behind her, on the

other side of the tree. She turned and tried to look over her shoulder, struggling to see around the wide trunk, but it was blocking the view behind her. She pushed down harder, trying to empty her bladder faster.

Then the sound again, like slow deliberate footsteps, leaves and twigs crushing underfoot. Definitely from behind.

She almost called out Martin's name, thinking it was him, fooling around, coming out to scare her or something. Yet, for some reason, she didn't.

A spike of apprehension pierced her gut. The footsteps were getting closer now, maybe only a few feet away.

Then they stopped, the person pausing, hesitating.

Karla suddenly realized how loud her urinating sounded, amplified by the stillness of the forest around her.

She contracted, stopping the stream, holding her breath too, trying to make as little sound as possible. Her eyes darted side to side as she tried to see behind her. There was someone there, closer now, right behind her, the tree trunk shielding them. Maybe they would walk right on past, not see her squatting with just a sweatshirt on and sneakers.

The atmosphere changed, the air growing colder, seeping toward her through the forest, not down from above as one would expect. Getting colder not because the sun had now dipped fully below the tree line, nighttime only a few moments away.

Karla began to shake, tensing every groin muscle, struggling to hold back her bladder. The person, whoever they were, had stopped, no sound now, but she still could feel them there, picturing them just a few feet behind her on the other side of the tree trunk.

They knew she was there. She felt totally exposed, her mind

crowding with questions only they could answer. Who? What? Why?

Then the ground to Karla's right darkened, a stretch of shadow thrown from around the side of the tree trunk. Karla jerked her head over her shoulder, gave a muffled cry, her heart sliding up her throat like she was going to vomit it up, arteries and veins still attached.

---

Martin sat bolt upright and stared through the thin nylon wall of the tent as though he could see right through it, his head swiveling toward the sound he had just heard.

"Karla?"

Fumbling on his pants and shirt, Martin stumbled out of the tent, dazed and confused.

The forest sat dark and brooding, the light almost gone. He had heard Karla scream. It wasn't a bird or an animal. It was … human. Her.

He took off at a run, making for the latrine.

Ahead, he could see the trail snaking its way through the undergrowth. He ran as fast as he could, calling out her name.

He had only covered the first few yards when something edged into his peripheral version, a flitter against the dull backdrop of greens and browns. He ran faster, ignoring what it was, ducking and weaving through branches, around fallen logs. Something smashed into his leg, sending bone-tearing pain up his shin, but he kept going. He knew something was terribly wrong, could feel it deep in his gut, sense it in the air all around him.

He was nearly there, recognized the shape of the tree, the wide distinctive trunk when it appeared up ahead.

Then, another scream, a piercing high-pitched, bloodcurdling sound that was almost inhuman. Not a scream for help, or in shock, or in terror. It was your last scream, the scream you let loose when you can't believe your short, burning-brightly life was about to end … badly.

"Karla!" he yelled.

Then Martin slowed, his chest heaving, his eyes wild with anxiety and desperation.

*Karla?*

She was lying on the other side of the tree, facedown, her red sweatshirt torn, hanging loosely off her back.

*Red?*

A dark blur tore toward Martin, cutting off his vision and the sight of Karla. He felt his body being lifted, then propelled backward until a tree stopped his momentum.

He dropped, collapsed into the dirt, his world tilting on its side.

He caught a fleeting glimpse of Karla's face, her head twisted toward him, eyes closed, one cheek on a pillow of leaves and forest debris. As Martin looked at her lifeless body, he knew all thoughts of a happy married life together and a family of their own were gone forever.

# Chapter 3

The last time she was there, he had lashed out in his drunken state, caught her on the side of the temple, nearly knocking her unconscious. As much as Sam had wanted to punch his lights out, she had resisted.

Instead, as any dutiful daughter would, she helped her father to bed in the spare bedroom, made sure he was settled, and placed a glass of water on the nightstand next to him before withdrawing.

There was something to be said about the high level of tolerance we had for family—and the low level of common sense we accepted in ourselves as a consequence.

Sam had gone home and cried while holding an ice pack to her head, waiting for the swelling to subside. Luckily, there was no obvious bruising—just on the inside. After an hour or so, her anger had also subsided.

Using her spare key, Sam unlocked the front door to her father's house and pushed it open tentatively. She paused on the threshold, darkness beyond, despite the fact it was midday. Taking a deep breath, she steadied herself for the known, stepped inside, and closed the door behind her. The air seemed heavy, had a certain texture to it, of lost hope, despair, and unrelenting bitterness. The light inside the room flickered; an ancient TV was on in the corner, the sound turned down.

Her father lay slumped in an old, battered, and worn recliner, empty beer bottles surrounding him. Thankfully, he was still breathing. That was Sam's biggest fear, walking in there one day and finding her father dead, gone without anyone noticing.

She found the remote and switched off the television and looked down at her father. Things never seemed to change despite the promises and glimmers of hope she had for her father. The disappearance of her mother had a profound and deep effect on him, in a bad way.

Clint Rubino at first blamed his wife, accepted what the townsfolk had surmised, that she had indeed run off with another man. But he was blind, unable to see that such claims were in fact not a criticism of his wife, but an accusation of his own shortcomings. She was too good for him. He was inadequate, couldn't keep her. Disbelief gave way to anger, then deep periods of resentment followed by bouts of jealous rage.

Yet no matter how many times Sam tried to convince her father that the rumors and gossip about her mother were just lies and speculation conjured up by those disappointed with their own failures, he viewed it as his own failing.

Clint Rubino bought into the gossip, the rumors, and then made the obvious connection that he was ultimately to blame. That it was his fault. That somehow his wife had suddenly fallen out of love with him, lost interest, was attracted to another man in the town. After a while, any strong and determined man would have caved in to the rumors and innuendos. You are a product of your environment. The more toxic the environment in a small town, the more likely that you'll eventually succumb to it and believe what you first thought was wrong.

Sam understood that when her father had lashed out at her, he was lashing out at his wife, her mother, at some image he had concocted in his head, his wife entwined in the arms of her new lover, his hands all over her, the man inside her, touching, tasting, and experiencing what Clint Rubino had once believed was only his to experience.

Moving into the kitchen, Sam found a trash bag in the drawer, brought it back into the living room, and began to clear away another day of drunken stupor. After placing the bag full of empty beer bottles into the trash can outside, she went back to the kitchen to tackle more mess. The kitchen counters were covered with a film of grime and stain, and a dirty cloud buzzed around the trash bin under the sink, which she promptly emptied as well. In the freezer compartment of the refrigerator, she found several meals, all untouched that she had brought last time. Sam felt a pang of sorrow. Her father wasn't eating properly, the drink and alcohol taking precedence over all other forms of nutrition.

He was wasting away. Sam didn't need a doctor's opinion to know this. He rarely ate, drank often, and almost never left the home other than to stock up on supplies of alcohol. What little retirement pension he had from working at the timber mill, was slowly being whittled away, together with his health, by the alcohol. Sam had lost one parent and was determined not to lose another.

After cleaning the kitchen, she returned to the living room and tried to wake her father to no avail. He just responded with a semiconscious rant and tirade, where Sam could make out her mother's name mentioned a few times. Making sure he hadn't soiled himself, as he had done last time, Sam took a blanket from the linen cupboard and draped it over him. It was best to let sleeping dogs lie or suffer a possible bite if you suddenly woke them.

Sam tidied up the living room as best she could and made a mental note to return tomorrow to check in on her father again, perhaps do some cleaning. Her father had decided long ago not to sleep in the bedroom he had once shared with his wife. At first he had. But as the years dragged on, and he succumbed to town gossip and rumors, despair festered into resentment toward Laura, and the drinking increased. Now he much preferred sleeping in the recliner or on the sofa in the living room or sometimes on the floor, where Sam had found him a few times when he had passed out.

Her father now never ventured into the bedroom, treated it as though somehow it had become poisoned, contaminated, despite the years of marital bliss. Looking back, Clint Rubino believed that he had been sleeping with the enemy.

Sam had left everything untouched in her mother's bedroom, and most possessions sat exactly where they had been the day she vanished. Her dresses hung in the closet. Clothing still in the drawers. The fact that Laura Rubino hadn't packed a suitcase, hadn't taken any clothing, intimate or otherwise, only fueled the doubt in Sam's mind that her mother didn't just wake up one day and decide to run off with someone else. She left the house one day with every intention of returning.

Time had covered everything with a layer of dust and sadness in the bedroom. Not cleaning or touching anything in there was Sam's way of never giving up hope that someday her mother would return, would resume the role of a loving wife and an adoring mother as she had done in the past. To pick up where she had left off as though her thirteen years of absence never existed.

Try as she might, Sam, even with the onset of maturity, couldn't, for the life of her, come up with a plausible motive as to why her mother had vanished in the first place. Sam's vivid memories of her childhood had not faded with time. Rather, they had intensified as she clung to every memory of her mother.

And when Sam couldn't find a reasonable explanation, and had dismissed the absurd, all that remained was the likely. That somehow, thirteen years ago, Laura Rubino, wife and mother, had met with foul play.

# Chapter 4

The sound drifted up to where he stood on the very edge of the escarpment. A canopy of forested green stretched away before him, filling the valley floor below.

The afternoon's light was almost gone, the horizon painfully bruised in shades of purple and red, and a rind of burnt orange moved along the mountain peaks.

He loved this time of day. The rotating earth seemed to slow and cool, creak and settle before nightfall. Sometimes shadows and darkness were needed to hide the things we didn't want to see.

Bright vivid greens were slowly fading to olive drab, gray granite melting into basalt black, the warmth of the day shifting to the deep cold shadows of night.

Then a faint sound floated up to him from the valley floor below.

He cocked his head as it echoed and bounced off the rugged walls, spreading then fading in the cooling atmosphere.

It could have been the cry of a bird, startled, then taking flight to the sanctuary of its nest before nightfall came. He couldn't tell. He wasn't an expert on birdcalls. He knew a little about a lot of things and a lot about a little.

He didn't move, just listened intently as the sound disintegrated among the breeze and the solitude and the raw expanse of the wilderness around him.

It was gone now.

Still, the man held his posture, his mind replaying the sound over and over again in his head. Forward, backward, stop, rewind, start again.

A skein of black dots appeared in the distance. They dipped then swirled into the valley below, ducked and weaved in unison before hurtling skyward again.

Maybe nothing, just a bird after all.

Finally, the man turned and walked back to the tree line and was soon swallowed up by the dense wall of green.

He intended to get back to the cabin before dark. It made no difference to him though. He had traveled this trail many times before in the last two weeks since he had been up there. Sometimes during the day, mainly at dusk to enjoy the final glimpses of daylight and watch the sun dip and die and the clouds burn like embers.

Others maybe would have been fearful walking through the forest at night, jittery at every noise or ghostly shadow. But he wasn't. He enjoyed the solitude, the company of the nocturnal sounds and incessant chatter, of the moon and stars. The night tested his senses and his navigational skills.

By day he would run through the forest, following old hunting trails, testing his endurance, his resolve, pushing his body a little farther each day until his muscles ached and his body was coated with a sheen of exhaustion. Then he would swim in one of the many mountain streams, plunge deep into the cold waters, and succumb to the bracing iciness as it washed away the soreness and tiredness he felt. The current would carry him past the churn of the small waterfall and toward a tumble of large boulders on the opposite bank. There he would stretch out, bask under the morning sun, the warmth of the rock on his back, the blinding glare in his face.

While he rested there, time slipped by without a care, the

world continued to turn without a worry. After he was dry and fully rested, he would trek back to the cabin, following the trail through the woods and guided by the fragrant smell of wood smoke. And there on the porch of the log cabin, surrounded by nothing but the wilderness, he would sit and drink the coffee that he had left warming in an old enamel coffeepot on the wood burning stove, and watch the forest shift and come alive.

Even when he had plenty, he would chop more firewood, add to the mountainous pile of split logs that lay against one wall of the cabin. He had enough wood now to power a nuclear reactor, not that he was worried about running out of firewood. Like his daily run and swim, chopping wood was part of the daily ritual he followed. It was therapy, something to occupy his mind, an outlet to vent. At first he bludgeoned the wood, hacked into it with silent rage. He saw faces and places in the logs, not bark and wood knots. Then, as time passed, he found his rhythm, his purpose, regained discipline and focus, and the blade cut deeper, the swing became easier. Afterward, he enjoyed the dull ache of worked muscle and bone. It tempered and settled his unruly mind.

The log cabin was well stocked, plenty of canned provisions. A friend, a colleague, said he could use it for as long as he needed. No questions asked, much appreciation given in return to the owner.

Sometimes he would walk back down to the stream with a fishing rod in hand, and if he was lucky, he would catch supper. Brown trout and rainbow trout were aplenty. After gutting and washing the fish in the cold mountain waters, he would then cook it on the bright shimmering coals of a small outside fire pit and sit under the coal-black heavens speckled with stars, eating his catch with just his fingers.

Simple and basic pleasures. Grounded contentment. Catch, kill, and eat.

Sometimes to relax and for sheer enjoyment, he would read by the firelight, by candlelight, even by flashlight. He was seeking guidance, direction, to reset his moral compass, which had been thrown so far out of kilter by recent events. He only had one book, battered and worn by the sun, dirt, cold, and rain. The pages were crammed with old bus and train tickets, but never a plane ticket, all strategically placed inside, bookmarking important pages and passages of wisdom.

Shards of coppery twilight slanted through the trees as he trekked through the woods, and minutes later the log cabin came into view, warm light spilling from the windows.

He was home.

# Chapter 5

Maybe he would just poison the dog, be rid of it, see how she would react. The prospect was certainly a tempting one.

But then she would get suspicious. Maybe call in the police, go looking for answers, and get a vet to do an autopsy. She would never let it rest; it wasn't in her nature. Like how she hadn't let her mother's disappearance rest for thirteen long years. She was certainly persistent; he had to give her credit for that.

And clever too.

At first he had underestimated her. Everyone in the town of Bright Water had. Over the years, he and others—the townsfolk—thought she would leave, go somewhere else. Move on and accept the fact that her mother had left her and her weak-minded father and run off with another man.

It wasn't totally implausible when you weighed up the facts: Laura Rubino, her mother, was an attractive, strong-willed, resourceful woman whose husband, Clint, was a loser. A no-hoper who worked all his life in the timber mill and got lucky when he met then married Laura.

She was too good for him, out of his league. She was destined to stray—everyone thought so.

Some of Laura Rubino's DNA had passed directly to her daughter, Sam, the fiery redhead with the blue-gray eyes, smattering of freckles, pale skin, and translucent pink lips. Mind you, the freckles had faded over the years as he watched her transform from a precocious, stubborn twelve-year-old into the twenty-five-year-old, tenacious, self-reliant young woman she was today. She was as bewildering to him then as she was to him now—a little more frustrating too.

He panned his binoculars left and right again, searching for the dog, but couldn't see it. Maybe it was inside the cabin. Maybe it was right behind him, watching him, silently, teeth bared.

His spine buzzed and he spun around.

Nothing.

Just the gentle upward slope toward the foothills and an infinite maze of trees. The forest silent, empty.

He resumed his watch of the cabin, his mind jittery now that he still couldn't see the dog. The damn thing followed her around everywhere. A few weeks back, he was certain it had stared right at him, despite him being well hidden in the forest.

Maybe he was just imagining it. But he felt certain those cold, dark eyes had glanced in his direction, searched him out against the backdrop of foliage.

The clouds parted, and sunlight cut a diagonal across his legs, illuminating him from the waist down but still concealing him from the waist up. He retreated farther back up the slope, hiding deeper among the low-hanging branches and leaves.

The dog was nowhere to be seen, and he was farther away from the cabin this time, but it still made him more cautious.

Maybe he would poison it after all. Then bury it with the others.

The log cabin was nothing special, but it was special to her.

A place of quiet and solitude, up in the foothills, a mile outside of town, next to a stream that crusted over with ice in the winter and ran warm and sweet all summer long. During the day, the sun would glint off the waters, and at night the moon would shimmer under its dark, rippling surface.

Sam Rubino had worked a variety of casual jobs while she studied to become a veterinary technician at community college. After she graduated two years later, she worked at a local veterinary clinic. The money was good, and she scrimped and scraped, saving as much as she could from living at home with her father and having a nonexistent social life. The hard work finally paid off when she had saved enough for a down payment to buy the cabin, which she was proud to call a place of her own.

Dr. Heck, the owner of the clinic, was fairly liberal when it came to allowing Sam time off to do her voluntary search-and-rescue work. He admired her passion and commitment. As knowledge of Sam's important volunteering work grew within the local community, new clients began bringing their pets into the clinic. The photo on the clinic's Facebook page of Sam crouching with Ghost clad in his bright orange search-and-rescue vest certainly had helped too.

At first, Sam used the cabin as a place to visit, a daytime retreat, to withdraw to when things became too much for her at home with her father. Ghost would roam the surrounding forest while she would sit, feet dangling off the crumbling back porch, wondering how she was ever going to fix the place up. But gradually over the years, she had. A lack of resources—money— had forced her to be more resourceful. She learned how to measure angles, saw lumber, hammer home straight nails, and paint without leaving creases. Little by little, she fashioned the cabin into how she wanted it.

It certainly wasn't finished. It never would be in her mind. But it was tidy, rustic, and cozy with exposed rafters, hewn beams, and plank floors. Inside, the décor was all throw rugs, secondhand stuffed sofas, cushions, and wooden furniture in need of a coat of varnish. The place had a lived-in, slept-in, dreamed-in feel to it that she liked.

And when things had become too unbearable with her father, Sam moved out of what had been her home since birth, and moved permanently to her cabin, with nothing but the birds, the wildlife, Ghost, and the faint murmur of the stream as company.

The isolation and peacefulness was the perfect tonic for her. She felt content, grounded, something that she hadn't felt in a long time.

She didn't entirely abandon her father though. She still checked on him when she could, brought him groceries and meals that she had made.

The land at the back of the cabin sloped gently down to the stream before turning upward on the other side, toward the tree line where the forest ran thick and somber for half a mile farther up to the ridge, the mountain peaks beyond.

Here, away from it all, time altered. The earth seemed to spin a little slower, the days a little shorter, the cold nights stretched a little longer.

Sam would rise at 6:00 a.m., like clockwork, make coffee using an enamel coffeepot on the wood burning stove. Then she would sit on the back porch, drink coffee, and watch as the sun bladed through the trees high on the ridge, the rays hitting the cold waters of the stream, turning it into a moving carpet of diamonds.

At night she would drink red wine in front of the fire, with Ghost slumped at her feet, one ear cocked, listening to the other ghosts outside in the night as they moaned through the trees and whispered across the tin roof.

A week had passed since she had returned home from

Madison County. Molly and Mary-Jane Cotter were never far from her thoughts. Despite trying so hard to remember the sisters in their best light, as precious family photos had once captured them, Sam's mind kept returning to the darkness she had seen in that cold, bleak forest, of what remained of them in the ground, images that she couldn't erase.

Time healed nothing. Only determination did.

# Chapter 6

Woody Valentine was a gruff, sixty-year-old search-and-rescue volunteer. In a past life, he was a marine sergeant who had seen active duty in some of the most inhospitable war zones around the globe. He walked with a limp, his penance for getting too close to an IED in Kuwait.

He was built like a locomotive, barrel-chested, all bone-hard gristle and muscle, skin like tanned leather. His hands, knuckles, and forearms were covered with a pattern of nicks and scars, more penance from a lifetime of stepping up when others wouldn't. His once brown hair had faded to ash, fashioned in a military, standard-issue buzz cut that he had kept since his first day at boot camp as a teen.

He lived on the outskirts of Bright Water, with his two dogs, *Lucky* and *Unlucky*. He figured that by naming the dogs as such, he knew the outcome of any given day when he was out searching with them. "Have all bases covered," was his motto from his marine days.

He considered himself lucky in that he returned home from the Gulf relatively unscathed. But unlucky that when he had returned, his wife, Meredith, had packed her bags and had moved in with his brother, Gus, who vowed that while Woody was deployed, he would "look after" Meredith in his brother's absence.

Needless to say, Woody and Gus were no longer on speaking terms. Gus and Meredith had three children, and Uncle Woody was never spoken about. Strange as it may seem, his dog Unlucky seemed to have more success, and it was his dog Lucky that had been unfortunate enough to have been hit by a pickup truck a few years back. The dog recovered, but the ironic name remained.

Woody had a fatherly affection for Sam, maybe because he could understand what she had gone through, despite Woody's wife not actually vanishing completely. And his fondness for Sam seemed to have grown more in the last three years, when it became obvious to everyone around town that her father had regressed into a reclusive drunk.

There were no small secrets in Bright Water, only people with big mouths.

Driving down the main street of town, Sam spied Woody's pickup truck slotted in front of the general store, with Lucky and Unlucky tethered in the back. She pulled into the parking space next to his pickup and got out.

Just then, Woody came out of the general store and saw Sam's old Land Rover parked next to him, and his frown turned into an instant smile when he saw Sam at the rear of his pickup truck, patting his dogs.

"Been back for a week, and this is the first time I see you?" he said, giving her a hug.

"I've been busy," Sam replied.

Woody leaned against the side, arms folded. "Too busy to even give me a call?"

Sam turned to face him. "I just needed some time."

Woody nodded thoughtfully. He had read in the papers about what had happened in Madison County. "I heard you did some good work up there. It must've been hard, being two sisters and all."

Sam just nodded. She didn't really want to talk about it. Her job was done.

Woody looked at Sam's Land Rover. "When you gonna get a decent pickup truck instead of driving around in that ancient British piece of crap."

Sam's Land Rover was from the seventies, spartan, welding seams and rivets visible, spare tire on the hood. In olive drab, it had a tough, no-nonsense military heritage to it that she loved.

It had been a source of frequent arguments between the two of them. Sam had purchased a few repair manuals for her model online, and like everything else, she had taught herself how to do some basic repairs and maintenance on the vehicle. She liked learning new skills; more importantly, she liked being self-sufficient, to rely just on herself instead of others.

Ignoring Woody's jest, Sam asked, "So what's been happening since I've been away?"

Woody made a show of thinking. "You know, Sam, nothing much happens around here. I had a call last week for a missing child, walked off from their parents' backyard. Turns out the child had wandered into the woods behind their home. It didn't take long to find them, and the parents were sure relieved."

Just then, a police cruiser slid slowly down the street. Sam took a step toward the curb, farther in between the cars, trying to shield herself.

Woody noticed this. "Have you seen him since you've been back?"

"Not if I can help it."

"Come on, Sam, don't be like that."

"It's my choice." Sam kept her eyes on the cruiser until it disappeared farther down the street.

Woody let out a sigh. "Would it hurt if you spoke to him? He often asks after you. He's a nice guy. And I know his father hasn't been well lately." Woody tended to be seen around town more, was more sociable, whereas Sam preferred staying at home, only venturing into town when she needed to.

Sam didn't reply, just steadied herself for the inevitable question.

"So how's your father doing?"

"He's doing fine," Sam lied, not taking her eyes off the street unless she was certain.

Woody looked at Sam with some skepticism. But decided not to push the point any further. "Look, if you need any help, you know where I am."

Sam turned back to Woody and gave him a forced smile. She didn't know what people around town expected her to say. That her father was constantly drunk? Had hit her on more than one occasion, and was permanently wrapped in a blanket of guilt and bitterness? Sam had tried to get her father help, had suggested he see the local doctor, or maybe talk to a counselor. Her father had ignored all of her suggestions. As was typical with most alcoholics, denial was often another symptom, convincing themselves and others that they didn't have a drinking problem.

"I just hope you're not still wasting time, Sam."

Sam had had this conversation with Woody many times before, where he had tried to convince her, like everyone else in the town had tried. Her mother was gone, had left for a better life. Woody hadn't been as direct and as outspoken as some other townsfolk. But every now and then he would subtly remind her not to waste time searching the foothills, and the forests, and the outskirts of town as she had done over the years. She just had to accept the fact, get over it, and move on with life. Things just happened that couldn't be explained. Sure he had been angry when he had found out about his wife, Meredith, and his brother, Gus. But over the years, he had come to accept it.

Over the years, the police had investigated the disappearance of Laura Rubino. However, they had found no compelling evidence that foul play was involved. The case was closed and put down as another disgruntled and unsatisfied spouse who left their family in search of a better life for themselves.

Sam never aligned with that theory.

"Like I told you before, Woody, I gave up searching a few years ago."

Woody studied her expression for a moment, then nodded, satisfied, and took out his keys and slid behind the wheel, the window down. "Come up and see me sometime."

"I will," Sam promised.

"And bring Ghost with you." He jerked his thumb at the back. "The other two would like to see him."

Sam nodded and watched as Woody backed out and drove off down the main street.

Glancing up and down the street, Sam couldn't see the police cruiser any longer. She began walking down the street toward her favorite coffee shop. Rounding the corner, she suddenly stopped and ducked quickly into the entrance of the store. Cautiously, she looked around the edge of the doorway and down the street.

There he was, walking toward her.

Sam ducked her head back. She was certain he hadn't seen her, but she needed to be sure. When she poked her head out again to take a look, he had disappeared. Sam waited for a few moments before stepping out from the store entrance and did an about-face and quickly headed back to her car, giving up on the idea of getting coffee and supplies for her father. It could wait.

Halfway between town and home, Sam glanced in her rearview mirror and noticed the police cruiser slide in behind her.

"Christ," she muttered, her heart thumping. She checked the speedometer, and she was doing right on the speed limit. She drove on some more, then slowed down. The police cruiser slowed as well, matching her speed before edging closer to her rear bumper, crowding her. Sam slowed some more and kept her eyes on the rearview mirror, hoping he just wanted to pass.

The police cruiser slowed further, and she could now clearly see his face, eyes covered by mirrored sunglasses, no expression on his face. Suddenly the police cruiser turned off down the side track and disappeared between the trees.

Sam gave a sigh of relief. She didn't want another confrontation like last time, just before she left for Madison County.

Bright Water was a small place. Difficult to avoid people you wanted to avoid.

# Chapter 7

It was the smell that first aroused Sam, the dusty scent of wood smoke that drifted toward her.

She had been out deep in the woods working Ghost, revisiting a location she hadn't covered for a while. Sam was climbing halfway up a slope, sheltered all around by trees, the midmorning sun slicing down from above. She paused, hand on a trunk of a tree, her breaths coming hard from the exertion. She could feel the base layers she wore damp with sweat clinging to her skin.

She pulled off her sweatshirt, looped it around her waist, then cast a critical eye farther up the slope. The smell of wood smoke was definitely coming from above. The only thing she could imagine was that a hiker had built a small campfire. It was rare that anyone would camp in this section of the forest. And hunters usually stayed on the eastern side of the canyon where the wildlife was more abundant.

Unless …

Pat Farmer's cabin was around here somewhere, she was certain. It had been a few years since Sam had been up this way when she had last seen it. Pat seldom used the cabin anymore. He used to work in the sawmill, with her father, until he was injured and took an early severance package. Now he spent his days in his house in town. Maybe he was up there now, taking some time away, hunting and fishing.

Ghost was preoccupied, following the scent of a gray fox, sniffing and foraging in the undergrowth. Sam resumed her trudge up the slope. The undergrowth and trees grew more dense as she pushed aside branches and twisted vines, until she finally emerged at the top of the hill. Through the branches in front of her, she could see a clearing where the sun shone bright and clear. Seeing movement in the clearing, Sam stepped forward some more trying to get a better view, dappled sunlight camouflaging her as she quietly edged forward. If it was a person, she didn't want to suddenly startle them, making it sound like she was a bear emerging from the woods.

Pulling a branch quietly aside, she looked into the clearing. An old log cabin sat in the background, smoke spiraling up from a tin chimney. However, it was what was in the foreground that had her immediate attention. Her eyes refocused, her breath catching in her throat, her mouth slightly ajar, her nostrils flared.

*Intriguing*, Sam thought, but not displeasing.

Ghost had silently made his way through the undergrowth and sat obediently next to her.

A man stood in the clearing, shirtless, an axe in his hands, swinging it in a glinting arc, followed by a grunt of exertion.

The air vibrated, the blade struck dead center, and the sound of splitting, then parting wood. Effortless, powerful, precise, one deft stroke. Another piece was placed on the block, and the process was repeated. Even from where she stood, Sam could feel the anger and anguish in each axe swing as though each piece of wood represented a lifetime's accumulation of disappointment.

The man had his back to Sam, and every strand and knot of muscle rippled and slithered in exquisite detail under his glossy skin.

Another lump of wood cut clean through. Then another. A huge pile of split logs, firewood, hugged one wall of the cabin. Sam kept watching, transfixed, unable to pull her eyes away, a tingling in her jaw from the primal rawness of it. Who would think chopping wood would be so fascinating? The man was like a machine.

Subconsciously, Sam propelled her feet forward some more. She tilted her head to get a better view, voyeuristic guilt rising in her that she hadn't felt since high school.

Sam blinked several times and came out of her trance. He must be renting the cabin, she guessed. No one in their right mind would buy it. It was too isolated, off the beaten path, at least a mile to anything that resembled a sealed road, and without the typical creature comforts city folk wanted. The man didn't look like a local either. Mind you, he didn't look like typical city folk. Didn't look like anything she had ever seen before either.

His face was still concealed, his back still turned. He placed another piece of wood on the block and swung the axe again.

If his face looked like the rest of him …

A branch snapped under Sam's foot.

*Shit!*

The man stopped mid-swing, stood a little straighter, then glanced over his shoulder toward where Sam stood.

Sam quickly withdrew back into the trees, retreating, not so quietly as she had when she had first arrived. She turned, started back down the hillside, Ghost at her heels.

She had only gone a few yards when she stopped, glanced back over her shoulder, uncertain which way to go. Forward or back? Hesitation clouding common sense.

Through the trees, the rhythmic sound of chopping resumed, drawing her back toward it, the left and right sides of her brain in conflict. Sam couldn't help herself. She turned and crept up the slope, toward the sound, against her better judgment.

Still hidden by the trees, she approached the edge of the

clearing again from a different angle, not the same spot as before.

She hadn't noticed the silence in the clearing until it was too late.

Shock gave way to dismay. The man stood facing her, staring directly at her. Sunlight hit him front on, illuminating him fully.

Sam froze as the man continued to stare right at her, no expression. Avoiding his eyes, she found herself lingering over his physique. No need to visit some faraway museum to witness firsthand Michelangelo's brilliance carved in marble.

And when she raised her eyes to his, Sam liquefied, forgot momentarily who she was, where she was, and why she was there.

# Chapter 8

The only thing Sam was disappointed about was the fact that he'd put on a shirt.

Sam looked around the inside of the cabin while Shaw busied himself in the tiny kitchen making more coffee. "Sorry for the intrusion," she said, not sorry at all. "It's just that this place had been empty for so long, I was wondering who was up here."

"No problem," Shaw said over his shoulder. He could tell she was snooping around but he didn't care.

To Sam, the place looked like someone living a very monastic existence, a self-imposed exile. Was he hiding out here? What was he running from? What had happened in his own life that made him want to withdraw from the outside world, to seek refuge in the mountains, away from prying eyes, and from human interaction? Turning, she noticed her reflection in the window, then hurriedly looked away. Sam couldn't help but think about her own existence, how similar it was to this, but her place had a more homey feel to it. Had she really cut herself off from everyone? Was she going to die a lonely person?

The place was spartan yet comfortable, functional. Truth was, after Shaw said hello, then invited her inside for coffee, she expected to see a mess, a man cave littered with beer bottles, discarded clothing, and dirty dishes. She saw none of this. Neither was the man a neat freak, like her. There were no books, personal items, nothing she could quickly glean anything about the man. Sam couldn't live without books, and it seemed that she needed to escape into them more often than not lately. She then spied a book, just one, open on a small rustic side table. She picked it up and read the cover.

"Meditations?"

"Marcus Aurelius," Shaw answered.

Sam jumped in fright and turned.

Shaw was standing right behind her, holding two coffee cups. He offered one to her. "He was a philosopher and Roman emperor." Shaw nodded at the book Sam held in her hand. "It's his writings to himself."

Sam said nothing, just stared up at Shaw. He was older than her, maybe twenty-eight. Quiet and unassuming, she gathered. Dark brown hair, brown eyes, and a rather intense, searching face. A certain innocence, almost boyish at times.

There was something about his manner, how he walked, how he moved. His eyes took in everything about her without leaving her face. Looking without looking. Respect, that's what it was. Most men Sam met—especially police officers—were glued to her breasts, like they were having a conversation with them and not her. But he was different, had a restrained confidence about him that she could feel slowly orbit around him like the menacing hum of high-voltage wires. Was he dangerous? Ghost didn't seem to think so. The dog lay slumped on a rug, head between his paws, his eyes watching Shaw. After a casual sniff of Shaw's hand and a scratch behind the ears, Ghost had decided quickly that the man was no threat.

Sam took the coffee cup. Good looks were great. Manners were a bonus. But a man with confidence was like a magnet to her. And he had all three covered.

Forcefully, Sam had to tear her eyes away from his. The book was crammed full of train and bus tickets, and Sam noticed a New Hampshire bus ticket marking the farthest page read.

"Why would he write to himself?" she said.

"Don't you ever talk to yourself?" Shaw countered, still holding her gaze over the rim of his coffee cup as he drank.

Sam tilted her head, appraising him, trying to work out this strange yet alluring man who was standing in front of her, like inches away, invading her personal space. And yet as she stood there, she felt no compulsion at all to step back, to pull away, and to widen the gap between them.

She could tell he was looking at her smattering of freckles around her nose, on her cheeks, across her chin. *Too many,* she thought. She was self-conscious of how her red hair, almost translucent skin, and soft freckles could make people stare at her. But he wasn't staring at her like she some kind of freak. It felt more like he was *admiring* her, how she looked.

"Sometimes I talk to myself," she said, stifling a smile. It was like he knew her, could gauge her, and yet he was a complete stranger. It gave her the distinct feeling that she wanted— needed—to know more about him.

She often did talk to herself and to Ghost. And at times she could swear that Ghost understood what she was saying, even when she was venting her frustrations about her father or with her search for her mother. Ghost would sit patiently looking at her, his head cocked questioningly. He tended to give her more attention when she spoke, more than most men had in her life. Certainly more than any boyfriend she had known.

"So what brings you to Bright Water?" Sam placed the book back. "It's not exactly a tourist destination."

"I like the peace and quiet. No distractions."

"Well, you certainly get that here," Sam said. "There's nothing much really around here to distract you."

"Oh, I don't know about that," Shaw said, looking Sam in

the eye. "There are plenty of beautiful distractions around here."

Sam's eyes narrowed, unsure what to make of the comment.

Shaw made a gesture with his hand. "The beautiful scenery, the mountains, the forests, the rivers, and streams."

Sam gave a knowing smile. She was not able to read the man's face to know if he was being serious or not.

"Where were you before here?"

"I was on Long Island."

Sam waited for Shaw to elaborate, but he didn't. She felt she shouldn't try and that he would tell her more if he wanted to.

"And you flew to Concord?" Sam asked.

Shaw shook his head. "I try to avoid planes. I caught the bus. Then hitched most of the way and walked the rest." Concord, the capital of New Hampshire, was sixty miles south of the town of Bright Water, which was perched up in the White Mountain National Forest.

"You hitchhiked?"

"People are really friendly around these parts. And I can take care of myself if needed."

*I bet you could.* So he has a fear of flying, she noted. That was unusual. Maybe it was his Achilles' heel? A chink in his armor.

"And town is only a mile or so away from here. I don't need a car, and I like to walk, take in the scenery."

"How long do you plan to stay for?" As soon as the words left Sam's lips, she knew she sounded like a police officer or a nosy neighbor. But they weren't neighbors; her cabin was at least another mile away to the east from here.

"I don't know," Shaw replied. "I'll stay for as long as I want. The owner of the cabin has been very hospitable and said he doesn't need it."

"You know Pat Farmer?"

"Friend of a friend," Shaw said, not offering more.

Sam looked at him, her mind ticking over. He was certainly a man of few words, guarded even. Yet he wasn't shy. Far from it. He seemed to fill the small space of the cabin, his presence, in a strong, confident way.

Part of Sam was happy with what Shaw had said, about staying for a while. No plans. No time clock. The possibility of weeks, not days of him being there. Not that she would've been devastated if he had told her he was leaving tomorrow. But it was nice to have someone of interest in the town that was staying and not just passing through. She didn't know how long he was going to stay, but she certainly brightened up at the thought of seeing a new face in these parts. Especially a face that looked like his. Sam thought it was strange he hadn't asked her a question yet, like it was one-way traffic, and she felt guilty, almost embarrassed that she seemed to be interrogating him. But she couldn't resist. She wanted to find out more about him. Who he was, where he'd been, and what he wanted here in Bright Water, of all places. In the wintertime, a lot of people came up to White Mountain Forest National Park for the skiing. But in summer, it was relatively quiet. There were various ski fields dotted all around the National Forest, places like Wildcat Mountain, Bretton Woods, Waterville, and Bear Notch. The entire place took on a different look and feel to it in winter—prettier, almost magical.

There was an awkward pause, and Sam didn't know what else to say. It was odd that he hadn't asked her one single question at all, apart from her name and the name of her dog when they first met.

Shaw went to the wood burning stove, picked up the enamel coffeepot, and refilled Sam's mug. It was a gesture that indicated he wanted her to stay, to talk some more. Maybe he missed the company of people. Maybe he liked her. Maybe that was too much for her to expect.

Then Shaw finally asked Sam a question. And it knocked her socks off.

"How was Madison County?"

Even the dog's ears pricked up.

# Chapter 9

It was the feeling you got when you knew you were not alone but you were.

Sam had that feeling right now.

She stood on the threshold, the back door of the cabin wide open behind her, Ghost by her side. The dog immediately dropped its head, hunkered down, and let out a low guttural growl, his eyes and nose twitching and searching, ears and corners of his mouth drawn back. Someone had been in Sam's cabin while she was out. Ghost was acutely aware of it as well. The atmosphere inside the cabin had changed, had shifted, displaced to accommodate someone else's presence. People tended to leave a residue, a trace of themselves after they had gone. Not just hair and fibers, but molecules of their character, their presence in the air where they had once stood, been. When your body touches the air, it leaves an impression on it—temporary, but still an impression, that eventually fades with time.

Sam slowly moved around the living room, her eyes running over every surface, edge, and keepsake. The cabin had been locked, and she was certain she had checked the doors and windows before she had left earlier. It was the first thing that she had done when she had started to renovate the place—fix or install window and door locks. Even though Sam had always felt safe in her cabin and in the woods around it, she had still been cautious. With her work, she could be away for days at a time, weeks even, if required. She didn't want anyone snooping around her home during that time. She didn't really advertise with the townsfolk where she lived either, and rarely had unannounced visitors. All her mail went to a box in town.

For the second time today, Sam went around checking doors and windows. They were all securely locked as expected. She went back to the living room and looked around, her eyes scanning up and down, checking everything again. Nothing seemed out of place, and yet she couldn't shake the feeling that someone had been inside, had walked around and touched, felt, and rummaged through her possessions.

She went back into the kitchen, uncertain what she was looking for. Nothing seemed out of place. The kitchen counters were wiped clean as she had done earlier. Her coffee cup and plate were in the sink where she had left them this morning. The coffeemaker stood cold and silent, its cord wrapped neatly around its base. There were no muddy tracks, footprints, or debris brought in from the outside on the floor except what Ghost may have traipsed inside. Sam had removed her boots and left them on a mat outside the back door as she always had.

Then her heart sped up.

In the small alcove off the kitchen sat a small desk and chair, where she kept her files and folders, research documents, and reports about her mother's disappearance. Someone had gone through the contents of the desk. There were just subtle things: A folder slightly out of place, pieces of paper askew. A pen moved so documents underneath could be read, the pen then placed back on top, but not as she had left it. Someone had definitely been inside her cabin, had searched through the accumulation of documentation she had carefully curated over the years. Copies of police reports, press clippings, articles of similar cases where husbands and wives, fathers and mothers had gone missing for no apparent reason. Different towns, different states, different circumstances. Same heartache and suffering left in their place.

Sam woke up her laptop. Thankfully, the screen was still password locked. The Wi-Fi coverage was strong up on the mountain, which was a blessing for her as she did most of her research online. However, she much preferred to print out and read lengthy reports, and most of her notes were handwritten, easier to spread out her thoughts and shuffle them around when they were ink on paper instead of pixels on a computer screen. There were some cellular dead spots deeper in the forest, especially in the canyon floor and down among the rivers and streams where Sam often roamed with Ghost.

Sam checked around her desk one more time. There was nothing there of any real value, except her laptop, perhaps.

No. Someone wasn't interested in that. They weren't that kind of thief. They were interested in stealing something more valuable: information.

Going outside, Sam searched around the perimeter of the cabin. It was too difficult to distinguish what had been disturbed and undisturbed in the undergrowth and forest debris. There were no obvious footprints, no trace left behind by the intruder. It hadn't rained for a few weeks, so the ground was dusty hard.

They were too smart.

"Maybe not," Sam said out loud to herself, contemplating the surrounding woods, thinking about what she had discussed with Shaw about Madison County. What he knew was already mentioned in the local newspapers, where he had probably read about the case and her involvement. Sam didn't elaborate in details about where she had found the two sisters and the state they were in. But somehow she felt herself opening up to Shaw about how she felt afterward. How it had affected her. And yet he was a complete stranger who had this weird ability to make her feel instantly safe, that she could trust him, that he would never betray her confidence.

Ghost followed Sam back inside as she went into her bedroom. Sliding out a bottom drawer, Sam dug under thick winter sweaters until she found what she was looking for. She pulled out a Ziploc bag, opened it, and slid out a simple white T-shirt. She brought the unwashed garment to her nose and inhaled the all-too-familiar combination of sweat, cologne, and distrust.

"Let's see how smart you think you are," she said as though talking to the T-shirt. Sam turned to Ghost, who sat expectantly beside her on the floor rug at the foot of the bed. "Let's go hunting, boy."

Ghost's thick tail thumped up and down, the sound vibrating through the floorboards.

*Chew toy time!*

Outside, Sam barely got to the bottom of the slope when she paused, Ghost by her side. Her cell phone vibrated in her pocket. She slid it out and stared at the screen.

It was Woody Valentine. "Sam, we've got a child abduction. Local police want a search-and-rescue team at scene of the family home to do a ground search."

Sam's heart tensed. Child abductions were the worst. Raw memories of the Cotter sisters came flooding back to Sam as she listened to Woody give her the details. It would take her an hour by car to get there. Forty minutes if she hurried. Every second counted with a taken child. She ended the call. Her plan to confirm who had been inside her cabin would have to wait. She knew who it was anyway. She just wanted to prove a point.

# Chapter 10

The first thing that struck Sam when she pulled up at the lakeside house was how deserted the property seemed.

She expected a hive of activity—the driveway choked with police cruisers, police officers roaming the grounds, the front path and door cordoned off, a gathering of curious neighbors on the street wondering what all the commotion was about.

She found none of this.

There was only a single police cruiser out front and a young police officer, who identified himself as Dwight Harris, leaning on the hood engrossed in his cell phone. Sam took Ghost off the leash, and he lingered by her side, occasionally straying a few yards to sniff the ground and cast his eyes suspiciously at the young officer.

Officer Harris was in his mid-twenties, gangly and long boned, yet to fill out into a manly solidness. He had the look of someone who had just been dumped by their girlfriend or an extremely bored junior law enforcement officer who was given the rudimentary task of house-sitting while the main investigation proceeded elsewhere.

Judging from the look Harris had given Sam as she approached, she felt it was the latter of the two dismal possibilities.

Harris proceeded to give Sam a rundown of the current situation, dictating from his notebook as though he was reading the obituary of a neighbor's cat he never liked.

Millicent, or "Millie," Walker had been abducted by her father, Kurt Walker, approximately two hours ago. Apparently, there was some lingering custody dispute. Alice Walker, his wife, had taken out a restraining order on him after they had separated six months ago. Due to his propensity for violence, the court had awarded full custody of their only child to the mother.

For Sam, it seemed like a distressing case of a disgruntled father who had been denied access to his child, and who had taken matters into his own hands.

Alice Walker had been severely beaten and was currently undergoing surgery in the local ER. Harris said that he hadn't received an update, but the injuries weren't life threatening.

"So where is everyone?" Sam asked, looking around.

Harris gave a resentful look, confirming her initial thoughts that he was on guard duty. Sam imagined the young police officer had a repertoire of various facial expressions, all of them despondent. "They're following up on leads. Some have gone by Kurt Walker's home and his place of employment. He has a white pickup truck that we have an all-points bulletin on."

"So why am I here?" Sam asked, struggling to keep her annoyance in check. Everything around Sam, the house, the grounds, the woods, and the shoreline to the lake, seemed ominously quiet as though whatever had happened here was unimportant; people and resources had moved on.

Harris shrugged. "Protocol, I guess. You were contacted to see if you could add anything additional to the search for the missing child."

"Abducted child," Sam said. *Typical*, Sam thought. Her talents and that of Ghost's were still viewed with skepticism. She was not treated as part of any major investigation, pushed aside, as she had been previously. Her presence there was just an afterthought, "following protocol" as Harris had put it.

"Has anyone searched the grounds? The surrounding woods and shoreline?"

Harris flipped shut his notebook. "There was a brief search done, maybe a couple hundred yards in every direction, but nothing was found."

*Of course nothing was found*, Sam thought. They had barely scratched the surface.

"I'm just here to keep a check on the property," Harris said breezily. He then looked pointedly at Sam and Ghost. "And to make sure no one disturbs anything."

Sam felt exasperated. She didn't know why she was there. The hunt for Millie Walker seemed to have moved on. She turned, and with Ghost following, made her way down to the shoreline at the rear of the property. The lake was a wide, deep indigo-blue body of water, unsettlingly still, silent and foreboding, the shoreline a mix of sand and pebbles that crunched under Sam's boots as she walked. For some reason she couldn't explain, she was drawn to this location, this spot first.

A small wooden jetty protruded out over the edge of the infinite expanse of dark water. She walked out to the edge of the jetty and gazed out across the lake, feeling the coldness of the water in the air.

In the distance, hugging the shoreline, she could see a scatter of other large houses, perhaps a mile or two away, a thick wall of forest behind them.

It was a peaceful, desolate location.

Ghost followed her gaze, his nose twitching. Sam glanced down at him. "What do you think?"

Ghost looked up at Sam with huge, dark, shiny eyes. Then he turned and stared back into the dark forest near the side of the house. His face stiffened and his eyes narrowed. There was no sound, no birdsong, no nothing. Like all the animals and insects had been sucked into a vacuum. Small wavelets lapped the shoreline.

But apart from that, the air was deathly silent. Morbid almost in its feel, it had an ominous texture to it. The hairs on the back of Ghost's coat prickled and quivered, confirming to Sam how he felt too.

Something was not right here. Looking farther back, she could see Harris. He was leaning lazily against a column on the back porch of the house, engrossed once again in his cell phone, thumbs working feverishly, an amused smirk on his face. Unofficial business Sam guessed as she watched him. She noticed a coarse rope tied to one of the jetty posts and picked it up. It felt wet. Glancing up, she saw the sky was a cloudless pale blue.

Sam made her way back to where Harris was slouching, her eyes tracking the edge of the woods she and Ghost had been drawn to before, almost expecting to see a person partially hidden among the tree trunks, staring back at her. But there was no one. Just an infinite myriad of trees fading into the deepening gloom.

"Do they own a boat?"

Harris looked up, annoyed at the intrusion. "What?" he said, his face scrunched.

"I said, do they own a boat? The Walkers?"

"I don't know." Harris went back to texting on his cell phone.

Sam nodded toward the house. "Can I take a look inside? I need something from the child's bedroom so I can conduct a search."

Harris waved her off with one hand, without looking up. "Whatever."

Sam rolled her eyes. Leaving Ghost outside, she walked into the house.

The inside of Millie Walker's bedroom was as expected.

A menagerie of pinks and pale blues, soft pastel colors, carefully curated trinkets and other girlie things. A small dresser and mirror sat to one side, a cluster of framed photos on top. Sam picked up one and gathered it was Millie and her father, faces pressed together, smiles almost intertwined as one. Happier days. But then again, were children at such a young age privy to adult turmoil that was present in a fractured household? Sam placed the photo back, thinking it strange that there was not a photo of Millie with her mother.

Sam's eyes drifted to a bright pink, plastic, fold-out makeup set. She smiled at the sight of the miniature foundation, eye shadow, and lip brushes, perfect for tiny, eager hands. Her gut tightened as her fingers drifted over then touched the palette of glitter eye shadows and waxy lip glosses in stark bright colors. Innocence and näiveté yet to breach the mindful walls of womanhood.

Looking at the bed, something caught Sam's eye. Propped up in the middle of the bed was a small plush toy, a white unicorn with a rainbow mane, a blue horn and blue hooves. Picking it up, Sam examined the toy. The once snow-white fabric had worn to a dull gray, smudged with fingerprints, and what looked like food residue. One eye was missing, and the stitching around one of the ears had come undone. It was the only toy that Sam could see in the room. It was obviously a keepsake, something that perhaps Millie Walker had kept close by. Something that maybe she would not leave behind voluntarily. Sam brought the unicorn to her face, took a deep breath. Years of cuddling, caressing, holding, dragging, pulling, and throwing flooded her senses.

It was perfect.

Nothing else in the room look disturbed. Bed freshly made, the drapes drawn back across a small window that overlooked the backyard. From the higher elevation, the lake dominated the landscape. Cold, unforgiving. It had an ominous, fatal pull to it, especially for a little child. On the left, the tall curve of dark woods seemed to have edged forward since Sam last looked, almost encroaching on the house like a spreading virus.

Sam looked down at the unicorn in her hand. "Let's go and find your owner."

Outside, Harris looked on as Sam walked right past him carrying the unicorn and signaling to Ghost to follow.

"Where are you going?"

Sam ignored Harris, kept walking, Ghost padding beside her, his eyes fixed on the plush toy in her hand.

Fifty yards from the house, Sam knelt down, lifted the unicorn to Ghost.

He sniffed the toy. Long, deep drags of invisible scent particles flooded his nostrils. Ghost gave a nod and pulled away, sweeping back and forth, scouring the ground nearby. After five minutes of circling, switching back, and searching around the perimeter of the house—nothing.

No trace of Millie Walker.

Behind Sam, Harris watched on with a bemused smile. He gave a not-so-subtle snicker, then went back to texting on his cell phone.

# Chapter 11

Bridget McKenzie had never liked living in Bright Water.

Her parents owned a local store for what seemed like an eternity. It had once been a prosperous little business, a typical mom-and-pop establishment that sold everything from propane gas to homemade pies cooked fresh from the oven in a small kitchen out back. Back in the eighties—well before Bridget's time—the store even had a small video rental section. Nothing fancy, just a few shelves, but you could drop in and pick up what was considered in Bright Water to be a "new release" that had been sitting on the shelves in the other big video chains for over twelve months. As time ticked by, and the world moved on, and VHS gave way to DVD, then finally succumbing to digital streaming and home delivery, the store and its now meager offerings remained stuck in the past. No matter how hard Bridget tried to convince her parents to move with the times, her pleas fell on deaf ears. Fast-food chains began to spring up around it, and big-box stores in neighboring towns, and soon it felt to Bridget that her parents' only source of income was under siege.

Townsfolk, born and bred in Bright Water, remained loyal though. But the river of cashed-up tourists and visitors that the store once relied on year after year, especially during the ski season, steadily dried up to barely a trickle these days as the people preferred to go to the big chain stores and new shopping malls.

As her parents steadily grew older, they began to rely on her more often to run the place. What had begun as a part-time job during her high school years grew into a six-day-a-week, dead-end job that Bridget could see no escape from.

After high school she had wanted to go to college, study graphic design. She was good artistically, had designed all her own tattoos that she had. Greg, the owner of the tattoo studio in Lincoln, had even paid her for a few of her original designs she had created. But it wasn't much. After she had turned eighteen, she had vowed to tell her parents that she wanted out, to leave the store, to take up her studies.

That was two years ago, and yet here she still was, behind the counter, stocking shelves, ordering inventory, tending to what few customers came in, and closing up late at night.

That was why it was a surprise when a stranger, a new face in town walked into the store and began browsing the tightly packed shelves. Bridget, who was in the storeroom in the back, only caught a glimpse of the man from behind moments after the bell above the door rang. But it was enough of a glimpse for her to subconsciously straighten her blouse and adjust the tortoiseshell hair clips that held her flowing chestnut hair in place.

As she waited a while for him to come to the counter, Bridget thought that perhaps the man had left the store, slipped out unnoticed. But then he quickly appeared again at the end of an aisle, his back still to her. Trying not to be too obvious, Bridget walked to the end of the counter, past the ancient cash register, trying to angle herself around to get a look at the man's face. Then he moved away again as though almost sensing her motives. He vanished down the hardware aisle and then partially emerged again, his face obscured by coils of heavy rope and plastic bottles of engine oil. He reached up with one hand and touched a row of axes that hung from hooks on the back wall.

She was about to call out to ask him if he needed any help when the front door swung open a little too quickly, banging hard against the wall as arrogant youthfulness spilled into the store.

Joey Lombardi waltzed in, smug-faced and narrow-eyed. He nodded at Bridget. "Bridget, you still working here?"

His surprise was not genuine, just overly mocking. It was a running joke with Joey. He said it every time he came in, rubbing it in a little more each time. He knew perfectly well Bridget McKenzie wasn't going anywhere soon in this town. Like most people her age in the town, she had no reason to stay but couldn't find a reason to leave either.

Bridget took a deep, fatigued breath, preparing herself for the cynicism that was about to spill forth from Joey's mouth. "I interviewed for a top New York design agency last week. They offered me a six-figure salary, plus medical and apartment on Fifth Avenue, with a view of Central Park," she replied dryly. "But when I realized I'd be leaving this town and not seeing your sorry ass each day … I turned it down."

Joey froze, not appreciating the sarcasm. He shook his finger at her. "I knew you would miss me if you left town."

*Like a hole in the head.*

Bridget glanced across the aisles but couldn't see the stranger. She noticed an axe was missing from the wall display. She glanced back at Joey as he sauntered up to the counter. He was soft and sweaty, just like his father, with beady, dark eyes, bad skin, and a reek of arrogance, entitlement, and cunning ruthlessness that no amount of expensive cologne could mask. Joey was the same age as her, but had genuine reasons for staying in Bright Water. Bright Water was that kind of place. As a teenager, you spent all your high school days dreaming of getting out of the place. Then when you trumped up the courage to finally leave, you spent the rest of your life trying to get back to the same town. Joey's father was Tony Lombardi, who owned Bright Water Ski Resort. Enough said except that his spawn, his only son, was composed of more than just the same DNA as his father.

"You owe me money," Bridget said.

"Owe *you* money?" Joey scoffed. He made a show of looking around the store before fixing a cold stare on her. "Since when did you own this place?"

Bridget could feel herself tense. "My family," she corrected herself. "Your account is three months overdue."

Joey licked his lips as he regarded Bridget. He had never had her even though he had almost every sweet young girl in high school. But Bridget McKenzie was one mountain he hadn't scaled. One fish that had dodged his net. Not from lack of trying, mind you. Joey leaned in, his eyes dropping down to the gap between buttons of Bridget's blouse, where a slither of pink lace of her bra peeked out. *Christ*, she's looking good enough to eat, right here and now. Maybe he could flip the sign on the door to CLOSED, then take her to the storeroom out back and discipline her. "Listen, Bridget," Joey whispered, his eyes still glued to the gap in her blouse. "I will pay my account when I'm good and ready. Money's just a little tight at the moment." He finally broke his gaze and looked up at her, a smug look on his face.

Bridget rolled her eyes, stifling a laugh. She glanced out the window to where a brand new, fully optioned, matte-black-wrap Range Rover Sport sitting outside. "Nice ride, Joey," she said scornfully, feeling slightly more than agitated now. "Must have cost a wad of cash, your new SUV." So typical of the Lombardi family in these parts, she thought. They had plenty of money, openly flaunted it, but took their sweet time to pay local business owners and contractors.

Joey followed her gaze, then gave her a sly smile. "Why don't you come take a ride in it with me? You know the back seats fold down completely flat."

Bridget gave a sour smile. "I'll pass on that if you don't mind. When will you pay up your account?"

"I'll get to it when I can," Joey replied breezily. Paying the McKenzie account was low on his list of priorities at the moment. Joey walked to the back of the store where the refrigerators were and came back carrying two six-packs of cold beer. "Add these to the tab." Joey started toward the door.

"You can't take them!" Bridget started coming around the counter—then she stopped.

Something moved to her right.

Joey stopped too. Both of them looked back in the same direction.

The man, the stranger, whom she had forgotten completely about was now standing there, at the end of an aisle.

In each hand he held an axe.

# Chapter 12

Looking back, it would all make sense.

The pieces of the puzzle would come together faster—in hindsight. Sam didn't know how she'd gotten to where she ended up, standing deep in the woods. Fragments of her memory were still missing even now, days later. The paramedic who tended to her after the event put it down to the blow to the side of the head that she had suffered. Temporary amnesia and all that.

And yet she had still gotten there.

She was chasing a ghost through the wooded darkness at breakneck speed. Branches whipping past, lashing out at her arms and across her face, trying to slow her down as she slipped and stumbled, the ground a greasy mush of black leafy decay.

Then she broke through into a small clearing, only to be confronted by an unfolding horror.

Afterward, she would reflect on the time line. Questions would push into her already crowded head. What if she had missed a green traffic light on the way to the Walker house? What if Ghost had paused for an extra few precious seconds in his dash along the trail, uncertain as to which direction the scent of Kurt Walker had deviated to? What if she had just given up? Given in to lazy apathy, like the ignorant police officer, and concluded that Millie Walker and her father were long gone from here?

The young girl would have died. There was no doubting that. But Sam had saved her.

It was the framed photo on Millie Walker's dresser that had triggered the chain reaction. The mild panic, then escalating fear. The photo of Millie with her father. Faces pressed together. Smiling. In the background, a construction of raw wood nailed into a familiar shape. Branches just visible at the edges of the photo.

Sam had run back inside the house, cursing herself for seeing but not noticing. Snatching up the photo frame, she stared at the picture more intently this time. The logic was in reverse. Kurt Walker not Millie Walker. Find him and you find her. She was important. Needed saving. Not from her father. He was beyond saving.

Sam tore back down the stairs, stumbled out onto the back porch, her head swiveling every which way.

Garage.

Inside Sam searched. Tools. Workbenches. Small glass jars. Rags.

Rags!

She snatched up an old T-shirt. Extra-large. A man's size.

As was often the case, old clothing recycled, repurposed for other domesticated uses. There was no evidence, articles of clothing left behind inside the house belonging to Kurt Walker. A vigilant wife and six large trash bags had seen to that when they had separated.

This time, when Sam gave the garment to Ghost, the dog didn't falter, didn't hesitate. Immediately, inside his canine mind, a mental bright line of scent snaked its way away from them, from the house, and toward the dark brooding wall of forest, the sight of which had unsettled Sam previously.

Ghost took off, the dog also sensing the urgency Sam felt building inside her, and vanished into the dark tree line.

Kurt Walker was calling. *Come find me.*

Ahead, Sam could see the powerful hindquarters of Ghost, pumping and bounding. Paws and claws kicking up mud and debris as he tore away from her, faster than she could keep pace. He smelled foe not father in the fibers of the T-shirt.

Ghost was too well trained to bark, to announce his rapid approach. He just ran true and hard, an invisible ground-hugging cruise missile devouring up the distance toward its intended target. Light footed and hungry, he danced over, cut sideways, and skirted around obstacles with effortless power and grace, his brain focused on just one thing.

Sam had never seen such conviction in him—in any dog.

Gasping and sweaty, Sam broke out of the woods and into the edge of the clearing. In the middle, a solitary tree stood tall and proud. Midway up, a tree house was fashioned around the wide trunk, the wooden platform supported by large branches as thick as a man's torso.

Ghost tore across the clearing, a low guttural snarl building in his chest, a funnel of billowing leaves in his wake as he headed straight to the base of the tree as though he was going to ram it. He sprang up the trunk, trying to climb, only to slide back down, his front paws feverishly clawing at the rough bark. Five, six, seven times he sprang back up only to suffer the same fate. Dogs could climb but not a pure vertical like this.

Sam's breath caught in her chest as her eyes tracked upward to the front platform of the tree house, which had no railing.

And the horror unfolded before her very eyes.

Millie Walker stood rigid, her toes near the edge, a noose of coarse rope around her neck, which was looped over a branch above. At least fifty feet to the ground below.

Ghost barked and frothed, prowling the ground below, eyes

locked onto the form of Kurt Miller, who was standing beside his daughter.

"Daddy, please," Millie cried, her face shiny with tears. "I don't want to play anymore."

Ignoring the crazed dog and the disheveled woman with flaming red hair, who had emerged from the undergrowth, Kurt Walker tightened his grip on Millie's shoulder and whispered into her ear. "Don't you want to be like Peter Pan?"

His hand then shifted, sliding around to behind his daughter's back. His offspring. His blood and DNA. To be used now as a cruel tool of infinite pain and suffering to destroy his wife.

Millie teetered over the edge of the platform as Ghost barked insanely below. Kurt Walker glanced up, making sure the rope was still secured to the branch overhead. They had built the tree house together. Father and daughter. Quality time together. It bore a personal significance to him, but more importantly, to his wife, Alice. Alice and Millie had spent countless summer days up in the tree house, drinking imaginary tea and eating invisible cake from tiny plastic pink cups and plates from a Disney Princess tea set. Because she was tall and had blonde hair, Alice Walker would play the majestic Princess Aurora from *Sleeping Beauty*. Millie would be Princess Belle, from *Beauty and the Beast*—and any of the other princesses as she saw fit. Because as a six-year-old, she made the rules.

The choice of location for Kurt Miller to carry out his murder-suicide was by design not coincidence. It would leave his wife's heart still beating but eternally torn in two.

What happened next were just fragments in Sam's memory.

She remembered seeing a rope ladder dangling to one side. But couldn't remember ever climbing it.

She remembered watching in horror as Kurt Walker pushed his daughter off the edge, her small body tumbling into the void, arms flailing, and a sudden, choking scream. But she couldn't recall seeing Millie Walker catching, then clinging on to the edge of the wooden platform with one hand, holding on for dear life, her legs thrashing about in the emptiness below.

She could barely remember standing on the platform itself, just feet from Kurt Walker. Then him turning slowly toward her, his rotating face being revealed one inch at a time, a mix of gloating pleasure and manic snarl. Then he swooped toward her, his menacing shape casting a shadow across her face and the world beyond. Then a crashing blow to the side of her head. Feeling giddy, blacking out, then awakening moments later to the sensation of being dragged along the wooden planks— toward the edge of the platform!

She remembered the taste of blood in her mouth, and her hair dangling out over the edge, her eyes clouded with tears, looking down, her arm outstretched, reaching down to pull Millie up. Then watching helplessly as the girl finally lost her grip and succumbed to gravity.

She had no recollection of her fingers on her other hand, searching blindly along her belt, finding, unclipping then springing open one handed her Kershaw rescue knife and plunging the razor-sharp blade deep into the right calf of Kurt Walker as he stood over her.

She did, however, clearly remember a warm stickiness engulf her hand and the high-pitched hysterical scream that followed. She thought she had twisted the knife into his calf, heard him scream some more. There were strands of memory of him reaching down, taking hold of her with one hand and drawing back a massive, balled fist with the other, ready to obliterate her

61

skull. But she couldn't be certain.

She could definitely recall his heinous, enraged face swelling in her vision. A pungent mix of his sweat, saliva, and nasal mucus dripping into her face, and then her withdrawing the blade from his calf only to reach up and thrust it deep into one of his eye sockets.

She remembered him falling past her, over her head and vanishing from view. Then hearing the sound of a crunching thud far below, like thick, dry branches snapping in two.

Later she would be told, Kurt Walker had fatally hit the ground—headfirst.

The rope from which Millie Walker was hanging from had gone still. So had her heart. With a bloodied knife in hand, the only thing Sam could think of was to cut the rope. To pull the child up by the noose would certainly crush her larynx and even break her fragile neck.

So she cut the rope.

A broken leg was better than a broken neck.

Sam vaguely remembered climbing, then almost falling back down the rope ladder, and staggering past the twisted, ruined corpse of Kurt Walker, to where the inert body of Millie Walker lay.

No pulse. No breathing. Seconds dead.

Sam would later recall loosening the noose from around the girl's throat, then pressing down on her chest repeatedly, careful not to break growing ribs and cartilage. Next, a cough and splutter of life as Millie Walker came back to life, her tiny chest heaving before settling thankfully into a regular rhythm.

Collapsing next to the girl, Sam could remember a cold, wet nose prodding her face, coaxing her to get up. And a heavy, coarse tongue sliding over one cheek before the sound of padded feet faded off into the background.

She was later told of how she was found. But there was no recollection for Sam of how her arm ended up being wrapped tightly around Millie, drawing the little girl's body close to her own, protectively, as they both lay on the forest floor.

Nor would Sam recall ever uttering a single, drowsy word before blacking out again for a second time.

"Safe."

# Chapter 13

For a moment, Bridget's mind went blank at the ominous sight. He had the brownest eyes she had ever seen. Dark hair, stubble across his jaw. He wore a checked shirt, sleeves rolled up, his forearms corded with lean muscle that rippled and tensed. The man's eyes looked straight at Bridget and then shifted focus to Joey Lombardi who, for once in his life, was lost for words.

The man walked to the counter and placed both axes next to the cash register. He slipped out his wallet and turned to Bridget. "I'll take these two," he said, placing cash on the counter.

Bridget paused, glanced back at Joey, then walked around back behind the counter and rang up the sale.

Joey didn't move, studied the man closely. He had never seen him before, and there was no other car parked out front of the store. He thought he was the only customer inside.

"Keep the change," Shaw said, before grabbing both axes in one hand and walking toward the door. He looked at Joey as he passed him before opening the door and disappearing outside.

"Who was that?" Joey turned back to Bridget.

"No idea. Never seen him before. But he paid cash."

"I told you I'll pay you when I get around to it, Bridget."

"Then, until you do, no beer. No nothing. Just because your father owns this building and nearly every building in town doesn't mean you can take liberties, Joey."

"Yes, it does, Bridget." Like most bullies, Joey's arrogance and courage had suddenly returned with the departure of the stranger. "And you better get used to that fact."

Outside, Joey looked around.

The man had vanished as fast as he had appeared.

Joey pressed the SUV remote, lifted the tailgate, and slid the beer inside before closing it again. He stepped back and admired the rear of the car. It hunkered like a beast lying in wait, hidden. His fingers absentmindedly caressing the smooth, matte-black surface, absorbing all light, reflecting nothing back. Dark-tinted windows. Carbon-fiber trim. Black on black. The only way to roll.

The SUV was a reflection of himself, his personality, the armor his father had counseled him in that he needed to wear if he and the family were going to continue to thrive and prosper. On the surface, appear dull, nonreflective, hiding not revealing your true intentions to anyone—ever. Always keep your emotions in check. Be mentally strong despite the fact you were surrounded by fools and idiots, people who were beneath your own station.

Joey had been, and continued to be, carefully tutored on the rules of life by his father, Tony. *Take everything, and give nothing in return.* That was the family creed his father had instilled in him from an early age. Friends. Girls. Money. People. It applied to all and sundry.

His father had pulled him aside one day and told him—soon after Joey had seen his father emerge from a motel on the outskirts of town late one night when Tony Lombardi was supposedly at a business meeting—that life was like a smorgasbord. "No grown man can be expected to eat the same meal day in, day out. In life, many tasty dishes will grace your table. Don't miss the opportunity to sample *all* of them."

Joey's mother had no idea of the indiscretions of her husband. Nor the pact between father and son. "Women are just a tool." More sage words of wisdom from Joey's father. "To be used sexually or to be used to fashion and create something else—you, my son. My legacy."

Recently, his father had divulged to Joey his plans to develop the whole town of Bright Water. Steamroll the place, expand the ski resort, and build a brand new hotel and malls on the foundations of the dusty, decrepit remains. He had shown Joey one night in his study, unfurled the detailed plans on his desk. Joey had stood there in awe, gazing down as his father explained what he had planned for the town. New shopping malls. Restaurants. Brand-new, five-hundred bed, five-star hotel. Mini-mart. Adventure Park with zip line and a world-class mountain-bike park to lure the extreme-sport enthusiasts during the off-season. From the detailed development plans, Joey could visualize it all, rising out the ashes of the old town like the *Game of Thrones* opening credits.

Joey patted the rear of the SUV, took a deep breath of the fresh mountain air, relishing what the future held for him. He glanced back at the store he had just walked out of and made a mental note to convince his father that when the time came, to demolish the McKenzie store first. Then the McKenzies and their teasing little bitch of a daughter would have nothing. They would all be swept up like the rest of the folks in the town and put out with the rest of the trash.

Joey couldn't wait. But until then, he would follow what his father had taught him. *Don't tell anyone what you are thinking, and keep your emotions in check.*

With his spirits lifted, and a spring in his step, Joey smiled to himself and walked around to the driver's side of the car—then stopped dead cold.

An axe was buried deep into the metal skin of the driver's side door.

# Chapter 14

"Describe him to me."

Joey Lombardi was sitting in his father's study, a shrine to masculine wealth and determination, clad in dark wood, silver-framed photos of coerced business relationships, and subdued lighting to hide past bad deeds.

It was going to cost Joey nearly five thousand dollars to replace the door on his SUV, and every cent was going to come out of his pocket, not his father's. A lesson in enemy awareness, Tony Lombardi had told his son after Joey had explained what had happened.

The blade of the axe had severed some of the internal electronics that powered the window and side mirror. The damage was done, and in Joey's mind, the retribution was about to commence.

Tony Lombardi took down the scant description of what his son could recollect of the young man in McKenzie's store. "I'll pass this on to Roy Beckman," he said, looking up from the notepad on his desk. "See if he knows who this person is, or at least keep an eye out for him around town." Tony regarded his son for a moment, a subtle look of disappointment on his face. Joey, like most sons who had been nursed at the teat for too long as a baby, was more like his mother than himself. He had hoped his son would have been better than this, taken care of the stranger himself. The kid still had a long way to go, and this latest incident gave Tony cause to question if his son could one day assume the family mantle. The local police didn't run the town.

Nor did the sheriff or the town mayor. Tony Lombardi ran the town, through a subtle and well-hidden network of alliances and carefully curated relationships that had taken years to cultivate. Could his son manage, then expand what had been achieved so far after he was gone? Time would be the judge of that.

"What else?" Tony asked.

"The McKenzie lease expires in less than six months," Joey replied. "I think the family is at the breaking point."

"Good. I want them gone, like the rest of them before we level the entire town." That was Tony's plan, to rack up accounts with most of the local business owners, then have them default on their lease rentals. The Lombardi family was by far the biggest debtor to most businesses in the town. Tony would drip-feed them a few dollars here and there, while the bulk of their account remained unpaid. What could the businesses do? Sue him? Threaten him? They all depended on him and his ski resort. Without him, the town would have collapsed financially years ago. So now it was time to turn the screws; get most of them evicted for unpaid back rent. That way Tony could expedite the redevelopment of the town faster, once most of the places were vacant. The demolition was due to commence in three months' time; county approval had been granted, which had cost him, but it was money well spent.

"And the timber mill?" Joey had been tasked with closing that down too.

"On the brink too," Joey replied. "Documents to repay the loan will be served on them by the end of the week."

Tony nodded thoughtfully. Like most of the other businesses in Bright Water, the timber mill, which had been there for nearly a hundred years, also had Tony Lombardi as its biggest unpaid debtor. It also paid to have a contact in the bank through which the timber mill had a business loan. A whisper in their ear by Tony that the mill was in financial difficulty, and before they knew it, the bank sent in an auditor to go through their financials. The bank would sell off the plant and equipment, and Tony had already made a separate side deal to settle his account with the bank, once they took him over as a debtor. He agreed in advance to pay the bank ten cents to the dollar. With the estimated proceeds from the sale of the hard assets of the timber mill and stock on hand, the bank would recover most of their loan, so they were happy.

Tony stared down at the notepad. "Anything else?"

Joey shook his head and left the study.

Tony picked up the phone and pressed speed dial and waited for the call to be answered.

"Mr. Lombardi?"

Tony smiled. He would have preferred "sir" but Mr. Lombardi would do.

"Roy, I need you to take a look at something for me, nothing major, just an insect I need you to find and crush."

Shaw was up at dawn and had completed the requisite trail run and river swim for the day and was back sitting on the porch of the cabin, drinking coffee and watching the forest stir and awaken around him.

For some reason he didn't feel like chopping wood this morning, despite having purchased a brand new axe. He had vented his pent-up anger another way yesterday, and somehow when he woke this morning, the animosity he previously felt toward the world had faded away.

He contemplated heading deeper into the valley or up higher

into the mountains, grabbing his pack and a few supplies, and just seeing what was there. Maybe spend a night camped out under the stars, build a fire, and lay out a sleeping bag. He thought about Sam Rubino. She was as reclusive as he was. Her cabin must be close by, and she had managed to find where he lived, so it wouldn't be that hard to find her cabin. But he decided not to call in on her, preferring his own space and pace.

Then he had a better idea.

He finished his coffee, packed food for the day, slung his pack over his shoulder and locked up the cabin before taking off into the woods, choosing a direction based on memory.

An hour later, Shaw was standing in front of a six-foot wire fence, with a metal sign that read, Bright Water Ski Resort— Lombardi Inc. It didn't take long for him to find a weak point in the fence, a section where the wire had rusted near a post that could easily be peeled back. Once through the fence, he walked only a few yards into the woods before coming across a well-worn trail up the slope.

The trail snaked its way through the trees and undergrowth, until the forest thinned, then opened on to a wide channel of flat cleared ground that ran up the mountain. A ski lift, still and silent, ran its way up the mountainside, with tall concrete columns.

It was strange to see it not moving, powered down at the end of last ski season. In a few months, the side of the mountain would be blanketed in snow, and the ski lift would be operating all day, feet with thin skis attached dangling below the lift chairs, the hum of the electric motors as people were pulled up the mountain and deposited at the top.

Keeping to the edge of the forest, Shaw continued upward. Farther up the slope, in the distance, he could see a tall structure of the ski lift station where skiers would disembark. To one side was a sprawling complex of glass and steel.

Two hundred yards up the hillside, a small shed was nestled among the undergrowth. It had a red warning sign with a lightning bolt. It was an auxiliary power junction that boosted power to the chairlift. Several of these were dotted up and down the mountain, making sure power was supplied evenly to the electric motors to power the bull wheel at both ends. Shaw walked past the shed, then stopped, turned, and looked back at it. The door was padlocked. Shaw continued until he reached the ski lift station.

Passing the station, Shaw followed the path that opened into a small cluster of stores, all closed for the summer. There was a café, first-aid station, and a bar with a deck that stretched out over the cliff drop off. Ski racks lay empty, windows were dark, and chairs and tables were stacked and covered.

The whole place was eerily still, undisturbed. It was hard to imagine the place at the peak of winter. Like the ski lift, the place looked dormant, in hibernation, waiting for the snow and the tourists to return. It would be another month or so before maintenance contractors would descend on the resort, getting the place ready for the coming season. But until then, it was a ghost resort.

Shaw turned and was about to start the journey back down the mountain, when something caught his eye.

# Chapter 15

For three days she saw no one, spoke to no one, and ate very little.

Sam went into hibernation, withdrew to the safe sanctuary of familiarity—her cabin. She shut herself off from the outside world. Her laptop went untouched. Her cell phone went unanswered. Momentarily, the world kept turning without her in it.

Ghost knew something was wrong. So he never left her side, following Sam patiently wherever she went inside the cabin. And when she did venture outside to give Ghost a reprieve from the claustrophobic heaviness that lingered inside, he ran among the surrounding woods; she would travel no farther than the back porch, where she would sit, her feet dangling off the edge, her elbows resting on the rail, her chin resting on her hands.

She saw the forest, the trees, the dirt, the rocks, heard the sounds of the stream, the patter of paws, the crackle of twigs and dry leaves as Ghost weaved and ducked and sniffed and prodded with his snout. Yet the stillness and beauty of Mother Nature could not pull her out from the dark well of guilt she had fallen into.

She had never killed anyone. Her father had taken her out into the foothills to teach her how to shoot when she was younger. He told her it was like driving a stick shift. Hard at first to master the fundamentals, but once you did, you could basically pick up any handgun, and stop any threat to save yourself and others. But using her rescue knife was a totally different matter. It was up close and personal, skin on skin, their warm blood on you. Despite the brutality of what she had done, Sam knew she would very likely be dead now—so would Millie Walker—if she hadn't acted.

She had given statements in the aftermath, been interrogated for nearly six hours, and then let go. It was clearly a case of self-defense. But that didn't make the bitter taste any sweeter.

*Kill the father to save the child.* That's how she had reasoned it. *Sacrifice the father. Innocent versus the not so innocent.* The mother would recover in the hospital, incidental injuries, and collateral damage from a lifetime of abuse. Well, that had ended now. Sam had made damn sure of that. Mother and daughter safe. So why did she still feel so bad?

Perhaps she could have, or should have, done something sooner, quicker; perhaps, the outcome would have been different. But she had no gun; she wasn't armed, and Ghost—God bless him—had made a valiant effort even though he was not trained as an attack dog.

It was midmorning on the third day of her self-imposed exile when the knock on the cabin door came.

Ghost didn't bark, simply got up from the floor at Sam's feet, padded over to the door of the cabin, dropped his head, and ran his nose along the bottom, picking up the scent that was carried by the draft under the door.

He sat back on his haunches, tail wagging. Friend not foe.

Reluctantly Sam pulled herself up out of the indent in the sofa she had occupied for the last three days and opened the cabin door.

Shaw stood in the doorway. His eyes looked her up and down, trying not to pass judgment on the disheveled state she was in. Messy hair. Bloodshot eyes. Comfortable, lived-in pajamas. Bare feet.

*Crap*, Sam thought, suddenly acutely aware of how she must look. His presence was a blessing, however. It gave her the much-needed jolt to finally throw off the winter quilt of guilt and depression that Sam had wrapped herself in for the last few days.

"How did you find me?"

"I was out walking through the woods," Shaw replied. "It wasn't intentional. Just a different direction, a different path to what I usually take."

Sam hesitated, the door ajar, one arm across her chest, conscious that she had no bra on underneath her skimpy top.

"I guessed this is where you live. There's no other cabins around."

Still, Sam did not open the door any farther, undecided.

"I thought you could use the company. You know? Talk."

Sam's face hardened, more from shock but also from embarrassment. This was not how she wanted to be seen, someone wallowing in their own self-pity. "Well, I don't need the company." And with that, Sam closed the door in Shaw's face.

He stood there for a moment, staring at the closed door before turning and walking back down the porch steps. He only got a few feet when a voice called out to him. "Do you want coffee?"

Shaw turned back.

The meek voice came out from the wedge of shadow of the open doorway. Sam then withdrew, leaving the door ajar.

Shaw stood there for a moment. There was no offer to come inside, no words. An open door was good enough invitation as any other.

The inside of the cabin was gloomy, drapes drawn, the fire was going: the place in casual disarray.

Sam settled back into her favorite spot on the sofa, her hands fidgeting, eyes averted.

Shaw could tell she was slightly embarrassed as he looked around. Without another word, he went into the small galley kitchen, plugged in the coffeemaker with Ghost in tow. In the fridge he found fresh ground coffee. He filled up the reservoir tank and turned on the machine before returning and sitting across from Sam in an oversized chair. Ghost slumped back down at Sam's feet, two eyes looking back up at Shaw, almost pleading; *can ya do something to pull her out of this rut?*

Shaw noticed a map on the wall, sectioned off into various parts.

He looked back at Sam, realizing she needed to break the spiral of self-pity that she was obviously in. Neither of them said anything for a few moments, just stared at each other. Shaw finally spoke. "I lost someone."

Sam looked at Shaw, a dubious expression on her face. "And you want me to find them?"

The half-hearted attempt at a joke brought a smile to Shaw's face.

Sam had never seen him smile. Instantly, her day seemed a little brighter, the heavy veil starting to thin, dissipate.

"They died. I couldn't save her."

Sam sat a little straighter, swept her hair from her face, tucking some loose strands behind her ear. "Why are you telling me this?"

Shaw stared at his hands pensively. "I need to tell someone. I've been up here for a few weeks now and ..." Just then the coffeemaker spluttered from the kitchen. Shaw glanced into the kitchen, almost relieved at the interruption. Maybe this was a mistake to come here, open up to this woman, who was a complete stranger. Then again, complete strangers had become some of his best friends in the past.

Shaw got up, went into the kitchen, and returned with two coffee cups to an empty room.

Moments later Sam emerged in a fresh set of clothes and combed wet hair. Taking the coffee cup, she sat back down, tucking her legs under her and to one side. "Did you love her?"

The question caught Shaw off guard. It certainly wasn't the first time he had pondered the same question over the months since leaving Long Island. He had become very fond of Annie Haywood, had understood her plight, the predicament she was in, saw a lot of himself in her. She was a survivor, a loner, wanted no attachments. He thrived on the ability to get up, no matter where he was or who he was with, and leave at a moment's notice. There was a certain selfishness to it, but Shaw didn't care.

Thinking back now—no, it wasn't love. He had only loved one person in his life, outside of his family, of course. And she was gone too. Not dead, just gone, faded into the periphery. A failed relationship, thanks to him. A common theme in Shaw's life by his own design.

"You don't have to love someone in order to care deeply about them. To protect."

"Who was she?" He was a complete stranger, who was being nice to her. Opening up, like most men couldn't. He, like her, was having regrets, had been wallowing in a pool of self-pity, but somehow he had climbed out of it over the weeks being up there in the mountains. She needed to do the same. Stop feeling sorry for herself. There were people in far worse situations than her. She should count herself lucky.

"Her name was Annie, Annie Haywood. She stole some money from a crime family in Brooklyn, and they wanted it back."

"So she was a thief?"

As with the question about love, Shaw had also pondered this obvious conclusion. Being alone had given him time to think. "She wasn't a thief. She was just misguided, saw the money as a form of escape, of freedom. That and the fact that she used it as revenge against the person she had stolen it from."

"I'm sorry," Sam said. "I didn't mean to pry."

"Hey, I brought up the subject." He could tell she had the same symptoms as he had when he first arrived up on the mountain: brooding, withdrawn, depressed, and angry with himself even. They shared a common bond but for completely different reasons. Sam had killed someone, whereas Shaw blamed himself for preventing a woman from being killed. "I couldn't save her."

"And you blame yourself." Sam completed the statement for him.

Shaw nodded.

"Do you have a need to save everyone you meet?"

"Only the ones I care about."

# Chapter 16

After he'd wandered aimlessly for weeks around the beaches, small towns, and secluded coves of the North Fork, Shaw eventually made his way to the tip of the peninsula to the hamlet of Orient and caught a ferry across Long Island Sound to Connecticut.

From there he'd continued north through sweeping woodlands of oak and hickory, to Hartford where he stopped at the house of Samuel Langhorne Clemens, better known by his pen name, Mark Twain. Usually, Shaw preferred to circumvent the larger towns and cities. But on this occasion, he had been drawn to the iconic landmark home where the famous American writer and humorist penned, *The Adventures of Tom Sawyer*. With his literary curiosity satisfied, but still with a heavy heart, Shaw pushed farther north into Massachusetts, giving the cities of Worcester and Boston to the east a wide berth.

"What did you do during that time?" Sam asked.

"Decompressed. Did a few odd jobs here and there when I needed to," Shaw replied. "I'm pretty good with my hands."

Shaw mainly traveled by bus or hitchhiked when the path he wanted to take had no bus route. He never traveled by plane. A month after leaving Long Island and starting his nomadic trek, he found himself in Manchester, New Hampshire. It was there he decided he really needed to get lost in the raw wilderness. His mind was still in turmoil. He picked up a brochure on the White Mountain National Forest north of the capital, Concord, and decided he wanted the isolation, to be alone up in the mountains just to think and to heal.

"And that's how I arrived here. Some time back, a friend mentioned that he had a place around these parts, so I gave him a call."

During the conversation, Shaw didn't go into the exact details of what had happened on Long Island; however, Sam could tell it wasn't good and had left a lasting impression on him. Behind his eyes, she could see a certain hardness, a resentment as he reminisced without too many words, an internal turmoil that was eating him. He had been damaged, like a spring stretched too far, never to return to its previous shape. The real question was, what would his new shape look like? His temperament? Slowly, our experiences shape us, good or bad. There was a deep-seated regret in his voice. He had spent the months reliving everything over and over again, looking for a possible alternative, a different course of action that may have resulted in a better outcome.

Finally Shaw looked up, his expression changed, melancholy and remorse swept aside. There was no point in dwelling on the past. He had done enough of that now. "I've moved on, put it behind me. Being up here was exactly what I needed."

"So what are you going to do now?" Sam asked. "How long do you plan to stay here in Bright Water?"

"I don't know. I like it here. It's peaceful. A little quiet. But that's the appeal of the place."

Sam rolled her eyes. "Believe me, you will eventually get bored."

Shaw gave Sam an intense look. "So, then, what has kept you here? Why haven't you left? Moved to the city?"

Sam said nothing for a moment, contemplating whether or not to tell him what kept her here all these years, in the same town she was born and grew up in. There was only one real reason why she was still here. Nothing else.

But before she could answer Shaw, he stood. "Look, it's none of my business anyway." It was late afternoon, and it would be dark soon. Sam was surprised at how fast the time had gone just sitting and talking to him.

Ghost raised his head off his paws and regarded Shaw with a more obvious look of disappointment than what Sam had.

"Maybe I'll see you around," Shaw said as he moved toward the door. Then he paused and glanced around. He looked down the small passageway toward Sam's bedroom.

"What's wrong?" she asked.

Shaw broke from his focus. "Nothing," he said, feeling slightly strange.

On a wall, tucked almost out of sight was the map he had noticed before. He turned back to Sam. "I don't know what you're looking for or why," he said, "but I know you're looking in the wrong place."

He waited and watched from the woods on the opposite bank where he had many times before.

At first, the knife in his hand just picked absentmindedly at the tree trunk next to him. But as the time dragged on, and his wondering turned into seething jealousy, the shallow blade cuts gradually evolved into deep, wide gashes, leaving a not-so-small pile of wood fibers at the base of the tree.

*What the hell was he doing inside the cabin for so long? And who the hell was the man?*

He had never seen the man before, the stranger who seemed to float out of the woods like a wraith while he had remained hidden, waiting, spying on Sam's cabin. The stranger must have been hiking nearby. And yet he seemed to know where he was going, knew where Sam's cabin was. The knife cut deeper into the tree, his anger growing by the second as he continued to watch.

The back door opened, and the stranger emerged with the dog. How very cozy, he thought as he watched the stranger throw the dog a stick, which it dutifully fetched. So the stranger was a friend, familiar both to the dog and Sam. This was certainly a new development. Maybe an old friend? But it seemed he was living nearby. As he watched the game of fetch, he made a mental note of the stranger, his approximate height, weight, build, and look. Definitely not a threat. But still, if he was just visiting, his presence temporary, then there were things that could be done to speed up his departure.

# Chapter 17

Sam chopped onions and diced tomatoes while Shaw was outside, tossing a stick for Ghost to fetch.

She smiled as she watched through the small window of the kitchen what could be the beginnings of a "dogmance" between the two, surprised at how easily and quickly Ghost had taken to him. Ghost was usually very standoffish with strangers even friends Sam had known for years. He was overly protective, yet around Shaw the dog was different, like the tall, dark-haired stranger was a lifelong companion, a buddy whom he trusted.

She had convinced Shaw to stay for dinner and was making a simple dish of tomato sauce with pasta. She called out that dinner was ready, and when they came inside, both Shaw and Ghost looked slightly despondent that their fun had been cut short.

There was little finesse. They sat at a small table with their knees touching, and Ghost was content to slump in the corner, his eyes watching proceedings with one ear attuned to any outside sound.

Sam usually ate alone, couldn't remember the last time she had cooked for anyone other than the meals she made for her father to freeze and reheat. There was no wine, and Sam felt embarrassed she couldn't even offer Shaw a beer. But he said he was happy with just tap water.

As they ate, Sam stole little glances at him when he wasn't looking. He seemed genuine, easygoing, and not pretentious, unlike most men she had met over the past years, one in particular. He was thoughtful and attentive and listened more than he spoke. And when he did speak, he asked interesting questions rather than trying to make small talk, or worse still, drop subliminal messages about wanting to get into Sam's pants.

As late afternoon slipped unnoticed into early evening, Sam found herself opening up more until finally the subject about why she was still living in Bright Water resurfaced again. There was no easy way to broach the subject. Sam was blunt and direct. "My mother disappeared thirteen years ago. My father and most of the townsfolk around here believe she ran off with another man." Sam paused, then said defiantly, "But I don't believe that theory."

Shaw said nothing for a moment. Finally, he spoke. "So you've stayed in this town for thirteen years to prove them wrong?"

Sam nodded. No one had quite put it that way before, making it sound like a personal, almost selfish crusade that she was on. But she was trying to protect her mother's name from being tarnished.

*Christ, thirteen years?* Had it really been that long? And yet Sam was no closer to getting any answers. Finding any tangible clues to explain the sudden disappearance of her mother.

"What do you think happened to your mother?"

"Something bad," Sam replied immediately. No hesitation. Total conviction in her voice that her mother had met with foul play. Sam went on to explain that her mother would never have left her as a child and how hard it had hit her father, turning him into a reclusive alcoholic.

"And the police?" Shaw asked.

Sam's face scrunched. "Next to useless," she scoffed.

They sat on the sofa now, drinking coffee. Sam had thrown another log onto the fire and had draped a shawl loosely around her legs. It had become unseasonably cold as the wind rattled and moaned under the tin roof of the cabin.

"So thirteen years have offered up little or no clues?" Shaw asked, trying not to sound disrespectful. It was obvious the young woman was driven and determined to find out the truth. Even if that meant accepting the fact that her mother had indeed gone off with another man, had left her only child and husband behind. Tens of thousands of people walked out on their spouses and partners every day for deliberate or emotional reasons.

More than once Shaw glanced over to the large topographical map on the wall. It made sense now. Sections of the map had been gridded off in a typical search-pattern manner. Despite there being hundreds of thousands of acres, surely, given the time span of thirteen years, Sam had searched the closest areas to the family home, the likely area of where her mother may have gone. Shaw concluded from the nature of the search, and the time that had passed, Sam Rubino was searching not for a living person. She was searching for a body, or traces of one, a partial skeleton. Memories and hope faded down to decaying bones. Maybe she had given up long ago on finding her mother alive. If she still held that belief, then she wouldn't be combing the surrounding forest, mountainsides, rivers and streams, and valley floor as she had been doing as the map suggested.

It was as much a devotion in finding closure as it was in keeping Laura Rubino's name unblemished.

Without asking, Shaw stood up and walked over to the map. Moments later Sam joined him. No words were spoken. For the next five minutes, both of them stood in shared silence, Sam's eyes seeing what she had seen and trekked a thousand times before. Shaw's eyes were taking in a new perspective. A two-dimensional rendition of the forests, roads, trails, mountain peaks, and streams he had no doubt walked and hiked through. Just a tiny area compared to the overall vastness that surrounded them. A red pin pressed into the map denoted Sam's home, the log cabin they were standing in right now, he surmised. Sam had started there, and had moved gradually outward.

"Where is your parents' house?" Shaw asked.

Without saying a word, Sam pointed to a spot on the map two miles to the east, on the outskirts of the township. The felt-tip pen that had marked that search area seemed more faded than other sectioned areas on the map. Especially the search area near and around Sam's cabin. In other words, the area around the family home had been well and truly searched. Numerous times.

She was definitely looking for a body; Shaw confirmed his first suspicions as he studied the map. She was moving east to where his cabin was. It would be where he would look—the more desolate and heavily forested areas.

But maybe she wasn't. Maybe Sam was just too stubborn to accept the truth.

"Before," Sam said, looking up at Shaw, "you said you didn't know what I was looking for or why."

"Now … I know what and why," Shaw replied.

"But what did you mean when you said I had been looking in the wrong place?"

Shaw said nothing for a moment. Then he indicated to the map. "Don't search where you can search," he said.

Sam frowned at the cryptic comment.

Shaw gave a slight smile, seeing confusion in her eyes. "Search where you *can't* search."

"Still not getting it," Sam said impatiently.

"Think about it," Shaw replied. "It's better to figure out the answer rather than having it spoon-fed to you. I've given you a clue."

Sam focused her attention back on the map yet still couldn't see what he had meant. She had being staring at the same picture for years, but nothing new came into focus or revealed itself.

"It's not on the map. It's what you know already."

Sam took a deep breath, turning over Shaw's words in her head. *Search where you can't search.* "Where *can't* I search?" Sam repeated to herself. Then her eyes went wide, and so did Shaw's smile.

"Now you see."

"Here." Sam's finger tapped a clear section of the map, unmarked, untouched by felt-tip pen or Sam's feet or Ghost's paws.

An area she had deliberately passed over.

"Why haven't you searched there?" Shaw asked. There were no markings on the map indicating why that particular section was off-limits.

"It's private property."

"So?"

"There are signs. Keep Out. Trespassers Will Be Shot."

"Just a deterrent," Shaw replied. "No one is actually going to shoot you if you are unarmed. Just idle threats and false bravado." Shaw leaned in closer and looked at the area Sam had excluded from her search. "I'm not saying break into someone's house. Just take a look at the land there. Search the grounds, the woods. That's all."

"Crap," Sam mumbled under her breath, realizing the mistake she had made. A fresh set of eyes were needed, and Shaw had certainly provided them.

"Is the place fenced off?" Shaw asked. "Completely? With guard towers and nasty dogs?"

"No. Just a few signs on wooden stakes driven into the

ground, warning people to keep out."

"So it's privately owned, not some government secret installation?"

Sam nodded, angry with herself for not seeing the obvious.

"It shouldn't stop you from looking, should it? More often than not, such signs are not to keep people out."

"Then what?"

Shaw smiled, speaking from past experience. "To hide something."

# Chapter 18

For reasons that would become clear to Sam, Shaw said that it was best to take a look at the area now, tonight.

Something about dark, stealthy deeds are best done under the cover of darkness. Taking Ghost, however, was not an option. Sam agreed, preferring to leave Ghost at home to guard the cabin, especially given what had happened earlier when Sam felt someone had been there when she had been away.

Sam gave Shaw a "don't ask" look when she handed him a man's hooded jacket.

So they set off with the cabin lights blazing, and the fire in the woodstove slowly receding down to smoldering orange coals. Outside was cold and brisk, the treetops silhouetted against the dark sky smudged with stars. With one flashlight between them, Sam led the way, Shaw following in her wake. She wasn't wrong when she said she could navigate to the location blindfolded. Long, confident strides, the beam of the flashlight held low, as Sam threaded her way through the woods, not looking back once to see if Shaw was there behind her.

After thirty minutes of brisk hiking, they emerged near the edge of a clearing on a flat plateau. A sprawling ranch house was at the far end, a warm yellow glow coming from its windows.

There was enough moonlight, so Sam switched off the flashlight.

An old pickup truck sat nestled under an outside awning near the house, and a spiral of wood smoke drifted up into the night air.

"So who lives here?" Shaw whispered in the shadows.

Sam nodded at what Shaw was wearing. "The person who owns that jacket."

Shaw looked down at the hooded jacket. "I suppose I could just knock on the door," he said. "Act as though I'm returning it to its rightful owner."

Sam gave a slight smile. "I don't think that would go over very well at all."

"Past acquaintance?" Shaw offered.

"Well and truly *past*."

Shaw waited for more.

"This is Floyd Beckman's property. I was engaged to his son, Roy, who lives here as well."

"I see."

"Roy and I were engaged for two years."

"So your ex-fiancé lives here with his father?"

"Correct," Sam answered. "Roy is the sheriff of Bright Water. His father was sheriff before him."

"Family tradition," Shaw commented. He remembered what he had seen earlier up at the ski resort but decided not to say anything yet.

"Handed the mantle down to his son," Sam continued. "That would've been maybe five years ago. Since then, his father, Floyd, has been retired. Stays pretty much at home. I think he has Alzheimer's from what Roy told me in the past. But he doesn't like to talk about it."

"And what about Floyd's wife?" Shaw asked. "Roy's mother."

"She passed away some time back," Sam replied. "A long illness, I believe. Roy never really spoke about his mother, and I never really saw her that much either."

"But you knew Roy Beckman, before he was made sheriff, up until five years ago?"

Sam nodded. "Been here all his life, like me. We grew up together. Went to the same school and all that. But we weren't childhood sweethearts, if that's what you're thinking."

"How long was Floyd Beckman sheriff of this town?"

"Since before I was born. I've only known two sheriffs in this town, the town I've spent my whole life in, and they both have the surname, Beckman."

This wasn't uncommon, especially in places like this. It was almost a tradition that the son of a small-town sheriff would follow in their father's footsteps. Because that was all a son knew growing up. Countless hours spent at the dinner table each evening, listening to his father recall the day. Being referred to as "the sheriff's son" rather than "Floyd's kid" or "Roy Beckman."

The next question was obvious to both of them.

"So Floyd Beckman investigated your mother's disappearance?"

The muscles of Sam's face moved, became more acute, pinched. "Like I said, law enforcement around here is hopeless."

Shaw now understood why Sam Rubino had avoided coming to this place, to search this particular plot of land. It wasn't because of the Keep Out signs. He didn't need to ask Sam about who broke off the engagement first. He could just tell from her tense body and terse words.

"Have you ever been inside the house?"

"Never."

"Not once?"

Sam shook her head. "Not even during the two years we were engaged. Roy never once invited me home to meet his father, informally, that is. I think it was because I blamed Floyd, his father, for being sloppy, not being interested in finding out what happened to my mother. I was a very angry, resentful twelve-year-old, and that carried on into my adult years."

"And you still hold a grudge? All these years later?"

"I've tried my hardest to avoid Roy Beckman and his father."

"So you didn't want to ignite the situation by searching their property?"

Sam nodded. "Bright Water is a small town. But I'm good at avoiding people—if I need to," Sam said defiantly. "But not now." She gazed toward the Beckman house. "It's time for a new approach. Change things up."

They skirted their way around the edge of the clearing, keeping within the gloomy confines of the tree line while still keeping an eye on the house.

As Shaw stepped over fallen branches and slid between tree trunks, he couldn't see any activity inside the house. Twice he paused, certain a shadow had passed across one of the side windows, dulling the glow from inside for a moment. But he wasn't certain.

At the rear of the property, a large shed hunkered in the darkness, maybe a hundred yards from the back door. The barn was in darkness, but it backed onto the edge of the woods. They could approach the back of the barn without being seen through the woods.

Ten minutes later their backs were hard up against the dry, rough wooden planks on the back of the barn, the view of the house totally blocked.

"Shall we take a look inside?" Shaw asked, wanting Sam to call the shots, decide what they were going to do. That was important. They were her demons to confront, not his.

"Why the barn?"

"People keep all sorts of things hidden in their barns," Shaw replied. "Might be easier to take a look now, while we have the chance. Especially if we can't get inside the house, it would be a wasted trip."

That was true. Roy was extremely secretive of his father's place. Perhaps he was hiding something. Sam agreed. "I don't want to break in though."

There was no rear access door into the barn. The only option was to work their way around to the front to see if the barn doors were locked. But this would mean being exposed.

Anyone who happened out the rear of the house or glanced out one of the back windows at the exact moment they were at the front of the barn, would see them. But it was a risk they were willing to take. There were no exterior lights, but they waited until a scatter of clouds crossed over the moon. Shaw was about to move when he heard a sound behind him, farther into the woods. It was almost inaudible but there.

He grabbed Sam's arm, holding her back, turned, then looked into the darkness.

"What?" Sam whispered.

Shaw said nothing, just strained to listen, squinting into the gloom.

Nothing.

Maybe it was an animal, an animal clever enough to pause mid-stride, knowing it had made a noise, disturbed the prey it was stalking. No animal like that existed in Shaw's mind.

They crouched against the side of the barn then slid along, making their way slowly to the front corner. Closer now, Shaw could see that one of the barn doors was slightly ajar, the wedge of murky darkness tempting them inside. Another bank of wispy clouds cut across the moon, and they scuttled around the front of the barn and slid silently into the gap inside.

It was only once they were inside that they realized they had made a fundamental mistake.

Brilliant white light blinded them both in the face.

# Chapter 19

Under the harsh, raw light, Sam covered her eyes, the back of her mind imprinted with a flare of white.

Shaw's eyes adjusted faster, but not before he heard a voice.

"Hello, Sam."

Roy Beckman stood next to a portable halogen light stand, the bright bulbs angled directly into their faces. "Not like you to break the law, is it?" Roy turned his attention to Shaw, getting his measure of the stranger who was standing next to his ex-fiancée. "Who is this?" he scoffed, arrogance dripping from his voice. "Your new boyfriend? My replacement?"

Sam's eyes finally came into focus, the blaze of burning white fading.

"He doesn't look like your type," Roy continued, his eyes doing another pass from head to toe over Shaw before dismissing him as unimportant.

"You weren't my type," Sam said acidly. "And get that damn light out of my face."

Roy didn't move.

"She came to me fresh and innocent," Roy sneered. "Inexperienced too. But I soon changed that."

Shaw's eyes narrowed, intrigued—not surprised, just intrigued at the man who stood before him while his mind conjured up adjectives to assess him: Predictable. Primitive. Lizard brain.

"Get over yourself, Roy."

"Trespassing they call it, I think." Roy gave a smirk. "But I'm not going to arrest you both. Only because we were engaged—once."

Shaw noted sourness and resentment in his voice as he studied him. A touch under six feet tall, lingering resentment that he didn't quite hit a full six feet in height. This made him shorter than Shaw but heavier. Two hundred pounds, wide, pumping-iron bulk with close-cropped blond hair that stood on end from too much hair gel, and a sneer across his face, a mix of foolish confidence and untested swagger.

Bigger, heavier, stronger mass than Shaw. Not smarter though. Every small town or local neighborhood had a *Homo erectus,* like Roy, who bucked the usual trend of human male evolution.

Nothing new here.

Roy noticed the jacket Shaw was wearing. *His* jacket. Arrogance gave way to anger. The sight of someone wearing his clothing made him incensed. "Why is he wearing my jacket?" Roy said bitterly.

"You left it behind," Sam replied, her eyes filled with the same bitterness of dragging up a past she would rather forget.

Roy shook his head, like he was breaking from the temporary distraction. "What are you doing breaking into my barn?"

Sam glared at Roy. "Don't preach to me about breaking in. The doors were open—and you were in my cabin. You had no right. You went through my things."

Roy did a double take, his face scrunched. "What the hell are you on, Sam?"

Sam stepped forward, ignoring the glare of the light. "It was you!" she hissed. "While I was out. You sneaked in like a thief into my home. You don't live there anymore."

Roy turned to Shaw. "You know she's insane. Obsessed about her mother. Can't accept the fact that her mom ran off with another man and left her."

Shaw remained silent. This was Sam's history. He could intervene at any time, smack Roy Beckman senseless before he could blink.

However, it would weaken Sam, undermine her authority in front of Roy, and make her look like she couldn't fight her own battles. If things got out of control, then he would intervene. But until that threshold had been reached, Shaw was content just to sit in the background and watch.

Roy continued to lecture Shaw about Sam as though Shaw really cared. Which he didn't. "She's not into commitment. Lacks the courage. Too gutless." Roy faced Sam again. "Aren't you?" He shook his head slowly. "Like mother, like daughter. You ran away just as she did."

The threshold abruptly breached.

Sam pounced. A white-hot meteorite trailing red flames. Lips drawn back, teeth bared.

She was fast but not fast enough—for Shaw. He caught a handful of the back of her jacket in his fist, one handed, effectively pulling her to a stop before she could reach the gloating Roy Beckman with her balled fists.

Roy took a step back and laughed. Amused by the sight. "That's right. You get the picture," Roy said to Shaw. "Got to keep her on a short leash like that dog of hers."

Ignoring Roy, Shaw spoke softly to Sam. "Come on. Let's go. It's not worth it."

Sam took a breath, green fire still smoldering in her eyes, her cheeks as enflamed as her hair. At first, she resisted Shaw's firm grip, then gave into it, almost grateful for his intervention, aware of what she would have done to Roy if she had reached him. Sam's anger subsided a tad, but the animosity she felt for Roy Beckman didn't. He was a cruel and vexatious person, someone who took great joy in provoking others, then hiding behind the sheriff's badge he wore. All this and more about Roy Beckman didn't come to light until the final months of their engagement, when Sam was beginning to have serious doubts about their relationship. He had done a good job of hiding his true colors up to that point. He was like his father, Floyd. The acorn didn't fall far from the tree, as they said.

Sam stepped back, cursing silently for allowing herself to fall into the entrapment. This is what Roy wanted, to get her riled, to make her do something foolish, give him a reason to arrest her and throw her ass in jail. The ploy almost worked.

Sam nodded to Shaw. "You're right. Let's go."

Outside, Roy escorted them along the gravel driveway and all the way to the dirt road at the front of the property. A few feet from the entrance to the property, Shaw turned and faced Roy, removed the jacket and then held it out to Roy.

Roy reached for the jacket but not before it slipped from Shaw's fingers and fell to the dirt.

"Too small for me anyway," Shaw said with a smile, preferring to freeze to death rather than wear the jacket now. "More suited for a child," he added. "Plus, I think it has fleas." Without waiting to see Roy Beckman's face twist and bulge with maddening rage at the comment, Shaw took Sam by the elbow and led her off the property and away.

Ten minutes later they found themselves trekking back through the woods toward Sam's cabin.

"I'm sorry." The shape of Shaw loomed next to her as they walked. His presence was comforting, making her feel safe. Despite the cold air, she felt warm, almost like waves of heat were radiating off his body, engulfing her protectively.

"Never apologize for anything," he said, his voice almost

berating her but in a good way. It made her feel good. To feel the words as well as hear them. There was more meaning in it; his support gave her confidence.

They continued in silence, moonlight good enough to light the way.

He was like no one she had ever met, nor would she ever meet someone like him again she imagined. Because he would—leave. Go. She just had that feeling about him from the first moment he drifted into her personal space. Her skin tingled, but Sam knew it was too good to last. Like those of the rarest moments in life, where everything just seemed to align. An experience. A person. A moment where you unearthed something special that you knew would never last. That was what made it special—the fact that it had a shelf life, would eventually end, die, and fade. But you didn't care. You were willing to trade the present, the moment, for the crushing sadness that would come.

Then you went on searching for more of those times, hoping you could find it again, relive it again.

"I wished you hadn't seen that," Sam said after a while. "Or heard what he said. It's not true."

"Useless words from a useless person. You're better off without him. Below you."

If it wasn't dark, Shaw would have seen a bright smile spread across Sam's face.

They reached her cabin, the warm glow of the light from the windows seeping through the shadows toward them. Ghost had sensed their approach. His tail was just visible above the bottom of the glass window of the back door. A thick, fury wiper blade of a thing going back and forth in anticipation.

Shaw paused and Sam turned into him. She looked up into his eyes, his face in partial shadow. "Come inside. Get warm."

Shaw looked down at her. "I should get going. Get back to my place." Then he paused, uncertain if he should tell her. "Look, I recognized Roy Beckman, the sheriff. I've seen him before."

"Probably seen him around town," Sam said, unlocking the door.

"Not exactly."

Sam turned and regarded Shaw.

"I hiked up to the ski resort, the one owned by a corporation called Lombardi Inc. I believe."

"Tony Lombardi," Sam said, a little intrigued now by what Shaw had to say. Shaw was economical with his words. If he said something, it was only for good reason. "He owns Bright Water Ski Resort. He's filthy rich, but he's been bleeding the town for years. Owns most of the property around the place. I don't like him or his son, Joey."

Shaw nodded, thinking back to the incident at the McKenzie store.

"And you saw him, Roy, up at the resort?" Sam asked. "It's closed for the summer. Nothing happens up there until they start getting the place ready for the next ski season."

"I saw Roy Beckman and … Joey Lombardi."

"Joey Lombardi?" Sam scoffed. "No big deal. The two are alike. Thick as thieves and full of themselves too." Sam thought for a moment. Why would they be up at the ski resort? The place was desolate, empty this time of year.

"They didn't see me," Shaw continued, noticing Sam's eyes narrow. "But I saw them clearly. I saw Joey Lombardi hand Roy an envelope."

Sam glared up at Shaw. "What?"

Shaw nodded. "Roy opened it, looked inside, and smiled."

Shaw let the words sink in before continuing. "Unless I'm mistaken, which is usually rare, what was inside the envelope wasn't a Valentine's day card either."

# Chapter 20

One of the benefits of driving a matte black vehicle was that it melted into the darkness of night.

Joey Lombardi sat behind the wheel and watched as Bridget McKenzie closed the store for the day. He knew where she parked her little Honda hatchback too: on a dirt parking lot that was a five-minute walk from the store. She was a creature of habit, and he had been watching her for some time.

The street was deserted, and he watched as she turned and began walking away from him. Joey pulled up the hood of his jacket, covering most of his face, then slowly eased out of the SUV and slid in behind her, hugging the shadows when he could, avoiding walking near the yellow pools under the streetlights.

Bridget walked a fast pace, clutching her bag under one arm, her cell phone in her other hand. Joey slowed his pace, allowing the distance to widen between them. If she turned suddenly and glanced behind her, he might not as easily change direction, duck into the murky depths of an alleyway or under a building awning. Even if he lost sight of her for a moment, he knew where she was heading.

Up ahead, Joey could see the glow of Bridget's cell phone bobbing up and down with each step she took, like a beacon for him to follow.

Good. She would be distracted, would not see him approaching her in those final moments before he grabbed her. It was a practiced move Joey had done at least half a dozen times before on other unsuspecting women. In the pouch of his hoodie, he tightened his hand around the snap-lock bag that held a moistened pad. He wasn't going to kill her; that would be stupid. The town was a small place; people would know. He was going to take her, though, back to a place that he had already prepared.

He allowed himself twelve hours of fun with her. Once she regained consciousness, she would realize she had been stripped naked, bound, gagged, hooded, and trussed up, chained by her arms to a rafter in a cold room that stank of her fear and of her torturer's desire. As long as he didn't speak, his identity would remain a mystery, something that would torment her until the day she died. She would spend restless days and sleepless nights obsessing over it. Knowing it must be someone from the town. She would never truly feel safe again. That was the real torture of it.

Blindfolded, it would be impossible to recognize someone merely by the touch of their hands on your body. How they gripped, slapped, and twisted your naked breasts. The raw, dry pain of their fingers inside you, probing and searching, no orifice left untended. Then the feel of something else more intimate inside you, your mind, and your soul. A taint that could never be scrubbed off.

When he was done, he would release her, dump her on the side of the road, and she would be none the wiser.

Joey smiled under the cowl of his hoodie as he walked. Bridget McKenzie was going to be added to his list of conquests. He had everything ready and waiting for her, just like the others.

Bridget turned the corner of a brick building and made her way across the dirt parking lot to where her car was parked under the dim glow of the only light pole. Approaching it, she slid her cell into her pocket and took out her car keys—then stopped. She turned and looked behind her.

Maybe her eyes were playing tricks on her. But Bridget swore she saw a dark shape duck back from the edge of a building maybe a hundred yards behind her.

She took a few steps forward, away from her car, thought about calling out. Then decided not to. She gave a sigh as tiredness swept over her. It had been a long day, and all she wanted to do was go home, take a hot shower.

Turning back to her car, she pressed the remote. The light blinked as the car unlocked. Then she heard a sound behind her, went to turn again, but a hand wrapped around her nose and mouth, pressing down hard, stifling any scream. She felt her body slowly go limp, the odd sensation of her muscles draining of their strength, and her bones turning to jelly. She struggled, but powerful hands held her tightly. Her vision began hazing over, then all light was snuffed out.

Behind the corner of the building, Joey hid in the shadows and counted slowly to ten. Had she seen him? Did he duck back in time without her catching a glimpse of him?

Next, he heard a car engine start up.

*Damn!* It was too late. He shouldn't have let her get the distance on him.

Cursing, Joey remained hidden and watched as Bridget McKenzie's Honda hatchback pulled out of the parking lot, leaving a dusty trail as it swung past him, a dark shape hunkered behind the wheel. The car did a sharp turn, thumped over the edge of the curb and onto the road, its headlights bobbing up and down before accelerating off.

Joey watched it for a moment until the taillights disappeared. He turned back and stared at the empty parking lot. He had missed his opportunity. But there would be other chances to grab her. Next time he wouldn't be so cautious.

# Chapter 21

During the daytime, it was easier to spot the loose planks at the back of the barn.

Shaw had waited in the woods, keeping an eye on the house until he saw Roy Beckman dressed in his sheriff's uniform leave at around 7:00 a.m. Shaw then waited another twenty minutes, making certain there was no movement inside, before he gradually worked his way around to the back of the barn. It only took Shaw a few minutes to pry the loose planks free and squeeze through.

This time there were no bright halogen lights to blind him once inside. The barn was in relative darkness. Thin bars of dusty yellow sluiced through bowed planks, providing Shaw with enough light to look around. There were workbenches, old, reliable tools hanging in an orderly fashion from chipped and warped pegboards. Bundles of coiled wire. Hordes of old wood. Rusty cans of lubricants and paint thinners with peeling and burned labels from the sixties. An assortment of screws, nails, nuts, and bolts, held captive for years in tiny glass jars, cloudy with age and powdery with dust. A lifetime of discarding nothing, repurposing everything. An old Dodge truck sat in the middle of the barn, the hood up, a faded fender protector draped on one side, someone apparently working on the guts of the engine.

Shaw went about searching the barn, trying to disrupt the orderly mayhem as little as possible.

Then something caught his eye, bright red and sitting alone

on a workbench. It was a backpack, nylon, with multiple pockets, black zippers, and straps. Unzipping the top compartment, he pulled out a tight bundle of clothes, men's trousers, and a long-sleeve shirt, some dried food rations, and a wallet? Inside the wallet he found credit cards and a New York driver's license, with a picture of a young man, dark hair with dark eyes glaring at the camera.

Martin Fassen, resident of New York State.

Shaw searched the side pockets of the backpack but found nothing else. He slipped the driver's license into his own pocket, then bundled everything back up into the backpack and left it on the workbench.

He made his way to the front barn doors, wanting to take a look outside to make sure no one was watching him from the house. But the barn doors remained firmly in place.

Staring down through a gap, he could see a thick chain had been wrapped around the iron handles on the other side with a heavy padlock, both a new addition since last night's intrusion.

Shaw slipped back out through the gap at the rear of the barn, replaced the loose planks, pressing down on the rusty nailheads before making his way back through the woods. Then Shaw stopped. Something pulled him back, made him turn around and glance through the trees at the Beckman house again. The air was still. Insects hissed and a few birds chirped. The woods around him had a calm, tranquil feel about them. Yet as he looked at the house, he couldn't help but be drawn to it. Something unsettling felt hidden behind the shuttered windows, within the worn siding, under the aging iron roof.

He wondered if Floyd Beckman was inside, watching him. Roy had said his father was housebound, which likely meant he spent his day sitting in a chair, or lying in bed, perhaps only moving to go to the bathroom. Perhaps not even then.

Shaw did a complete one-eighty and began moving back toward the house. If he was caught, he could make up some excuse that he was hiking through the woods and just got lost. Floyd Beckham wouldn't know who he was. He was a stranger, unless Roy had told him. Then again, he wouldn't have described to his father how Shaw looked.

The back screen door was locked as was the front screen door, the place devoid of life, sat hunkered, dormant, in the middle of the forest that had grown around it. Undeterred, Shaw moved to the west side of the house, found a low sash window without shutters, the glass panes glazed over with grime and time. Taking a penknife, he slid the blade between the gap in the two frames and rotated open the lock. It took supreme effort to raise the window without splintering the rail. Neglect and lack of lubrication almost welding the two sections tight.

Pulling himself up, Shaw passed silently through and into the gloom beyond, carefully sliding the window down behind him.

Ghostly shapes stood waiting for him and Shaw tensed. Old bedsheets, yellow and dusty, were draped over the furniture, giving the impression of an audience of shrouded people standing and sitting, waiting for him to perform. The room was heavy with old pollen and dust and trapped air, like a crypt. The only thing that wasn't covered was a lamp that stood in one corner, its cord plugged into some sort of device, then into the wall socket. Crouching down, Shaw could hear the faint clicking sound from the dial on the face of the device. It was a programmable timer, designed to turn the lamp on at dusk and off before midnight.

Outside the room was a hallway. A once thick, bright red carpet, now dull and emaciated, ran its length in both directions.

He paused and listened, could hear nothing except the sound of ancient drywall and floorboards clicking and settling. Glancing up at the ceiling, he thought he heard something above, deliberate movement. Then nothing.

Shaw turned right, opened the first door he came to and entered.

A study. More furniture covered with heavy folds of material. An old rolltop desk that wasn't covered, sat against one wall. Another lamp stood strategically placed near a window, plugged into another programmable timer, set to the same time to turn on and off just like the other one he had found.

The next two doors were locked, and the hallway opened up into a large kitchen. Unlike the rest of the house, the kitchen was perfectly clean, the window shades drawn up, and not a speck of dust in sight. But the design was still frozen in time. Old laminate cupboards, a large ceramic sink, ancient linoleum, scarred and haggard from a million footsteps. The smell of burnt toast and coffee hung in the air. The coffeemaker that sat on the counter was turned off, but the flask warm to the touch. In the sink, Shaw found one plate, one knife, and a coffee cup.

The refrigerator sat humming in the corner, a mint-green monstrosity of pressed aluminum, steel, chrome, rubber, and plastic, built in a factory in Philadelphia back in the fifties by men with calloused hands, who drank beer, and ate steak that mooed, from an era where the only thing that got posted, was the mail. It had a chrome handle the size of a ice-skate blade attached to the front, which resembled the huge curved hood of a vintage Studebaker. Inside were fresh provisions, well within their expiration dates. Shaw didn't bother looking inside the freezer above.

Upstairs, Shaw found much of the same. Sealed rooms like

tombs, sheets covering everything, windows closed to sunlight. Trapped air and years of stillness. All except one bedroom that Roy Beckman obviously occupied. However, Shaw wasn't into poking around someone else's personal space or possessions.

What had become blatantly obvious to Shaw as he slid through the downstairs window before retreating quickly back to the cover of the tree line, was that neither Floyd Beckman nor any visible trace of his presence, was anywhere to be seen.

It was as though he never existed.

# Chapter 22

*I need to see you.*

Sam placed the bag of groceries down on the porch and plucked the note from the doorjamb, recognizing the consequences of someone not having an email or cell phone.

She smiled but for all the wrong reasons.

Thirty minutes later, Sam was sitting on the sofa in Shaw's cabin, cradling a cup of freshly brewed coffee in her hands, with Ghost circling outside like a surveillance drone.

"I found something," Shaw started once he settled in an old leather chair across from her.

"What?" Sam asked, not expecting the answer she got next.

Shaw handed Sam the driver's license for Martin Fassen, then told her everything—the red backpack, getting inside the Beckman house. "Can you do some digging on who he is?"

Sam twirled the small laminated card in her hand. Even if she had brought her laptop, there would be no internet reception this deep in the woods. She pocketed the license, wondering what had happened to Floyd Beckman.

"And you're certain the house was empty? As in, Roy is living there alone?"

"As far as I can tell. The rest of the house was covered up, dormant. Most the rooms were locked."

"So where do you think Floyd Beckman is?"

"It's not relevant. His son is lying. Maybe it's pride."

"Pride?" Sam asked.

"His father's health has probably deteriorated to such an

extent. So rather than telling anyone, Roy simply put him into a care home."

"So why tell everyone that he still lives there?" Sam had been pondering the question ever since Shaw had told her what he *hadn't* found.

"I'm not sure."

"But you are." Sam smiled.

Shaw rolled his eyes at the quip. "Find out who Martin Fassen is, and you may find your answer."

"I will."

A silence descended between them, making Sam feel slightly uncomfortable. Then she got the cue that Shaw was hinting at. "Now?"

Shaw nodded. "No time like the present."

Disappointed, Sam finished her coffee, placed the cup down, and stood. At the door she paused, an idea entering her head. "The town is having its annual end of summer fair," she said, looking at Shaw.

Shaw stood there expectantly.

"I go each year, tradition and all that," Sam added.

"Tradition," Shaw said slowly.

Sam nodded. "I thought it would be fun to go. You know, get out for a while." Sam needed some enjoyment in her life right now. To laugh, to be a kid again, and forget all the death she had seen recently. "It starts at dusk."

"Tonight?"

"I was wondering…" Sam let her words hang.

"Okay."

Sam smiled. "Okay?"

Shaw nodded. "But after you check up about Martin Fassen."

Sam left Shaw's cabin and hurried back through the woods

to her own, spurred on by what possibilities the evening could bring.

Back at her cabin, Sam powered up her laptop.

But not before checking the doors and windows, making certain no one had paid her a visit while she was out.

She first did a basic name search for Martin Fassen. She was shocked when *slap bang* at the top of the results page was a recent news article for a missing couple. Martin Fassen and Karla Brigan were a young, engaged couple from Germany who had gone missing a week ago while hiking through White Mountain National Forest. The German couple had arrived from Berlin, and according to family sources, they were backpacking their way up through the Berkshires, a rural region of Western Massachusetts, then on into New Hampshire. The news article showed a picture of them, no doubt pulled from a Facebook page, showing the couple taking a selfie perched on top of a large rock, the sprawling forest below and mountain peaks in the background. Bright grinning faces, young and carefree, with faraway looks in their eyes. Their last social media post was more than two weeks ago, saying how excited they were to be hiking through White Mountain.

Then nothing. No communications. Not a peep. They were supposed to be hiking for a week in the National Forest, then come out. But they didn't come out, or if they had, no one had seen them. Their rental car was found in the parking lot at the start of one of the less frequented hiking trails, in a more desolate region of the park.

Sam sat back and glanced at the clock, surprised that almost two hours had passed since she had first sat down at her laptop.

She was so engrossed that she hadn't noticed the light inside had faded to a watery gray, and the wood on the fire had burned down to cold, powdery ash. She shivered as she stood and grabbed a blanket, wrapping it around her, and then cursed when she saw the wood pile next to the fireplace was bare. "Come," Sam said to Ghost as she opened the back door to fetch more firewood.

A light mist was working its way down from the treetops on the other side of the stream, curling through the branches toward her. The sun had gone, and a chill bit through the thin blanket Sam had wrapped around herself. The log pile was on the other side of the cabin, and Sam quickly loaded up her arms with as much wood as she could carry, not wanting to come back out in the middle of the night to collect more. Ghost drifted off toward the bottom of the slope, then looked back at Sam with almost a smile of relief on his face as he cocked one hind leg against an often peed on, wilting sapling. The light was fading with each passing minute. Sam stumbled back around the cabin to the open back door, dropping pieces of wood as she went. Ghost bounded after her, ducking through the gap just before she kicked the door shut with her heel.

It only took a few moments for the fire to start up again, and soon flames were licking hungrily at a neat teepee of logs Sam had built up in the hearth. With the fire stoked and crackling, and a freshly brewed mug of coffee warming her hands, Sam returned to her laptop and continued her research. There was no further news or recent updates on the missing couple. Picking up her cell phone, Sam called Woody Valentine to see if he knew anything about the missing couple.

"Local and state police are still looking into it," Woody said. "They've got a state police K-9 unit on it. But I haven't heard anything. You know, Sam, they're pretty tight lipped. They see us as just a bunch of amateurs, share nothing with us."

Sam knew all too well the rivalry between the official K-9 New Hampshire Department of Safety, a division of the state police, and the volunteer organization that Sam was a member of. Despite a wealth of experience, local knowledge, and devotion of Sam's fellow canine handlers, they always felt like the poor relative or "country cousin" of their state and local police counterparts. Woody ended the call by promising Sam that if he heard anything on the mountain "grapevine" about the missing couple, he would call her.

The missing couple would probably wander out in a few days' time, a little dehydrated and weather beaten, wondering what all the fuss was about. Then Sam remembered the red backpack Shaw had found. Maybe Martin Fassen had lost it. Had placed it down on a boulder to capture a sunset or a sunrise with his cell phone, turned his back for only a second, only to see it tumble down the mountainside, get swallowed up by vegetation far below. Then how did it turn up in Roy Beckman's barn? Why was it still there? Why hadn't Roy turned it over to the state police? As Sam stood with her back to the fire, soaking up the warmth, her eyes looking at the two smiling faces on her laptop screen, she felt a coldness drift through her. Roy Beckman knew something.

She went to the kitchen and placed her cup in the sink—then jumped back in fright as a shadow passed outside the window.

# Chapter 23

The fact that Ghost didn't bark made Sam's heart settle back down from her throat, into its rightful place in her chest.

It was fully dark outside. Black as oil.

She opened the back door to see Shaw standing there, faded jeans, oxblood boots, and a thin, white T-shirt that was no match for the falling temperature. His frame seemed to fill the doorway. Dark eyes regarded her, his sheepish smile warmed her.

For a moment Sam forgot where she was. Who she was.

She would remember this exact moment. Would recall it when she was old and gray, thinking back on her life to those subsequent fleeting, magical moments that were so intense yet passed far too quickly. It was a glitch in her time, a stumble in her otherwise normal heartbeat, where she had stopped breathing, and in her mind, the earth had stopped rotating.

"Can I come in?"

Sam blinked. The needle dragged across the vinyl, destroying the vision of him over her, his chest crushing the air from her lungs. Sam stepped back, the reality standing now in front of her. "Of course you can."

Despite what he was wearing, Shaw didn't seem perturbed. With Ghost at his feet, he sat next to the fire, warming his hands and listening intently while Sam relayed what scant information she had discovered about Martin Fassen and Karla Brigan.

Then Shaw pulled something from his memory. He was standing on the very edge of the escarpment, the forest stretching away before him, a sound that he thought was a bird cry was drifting up from the valley floor to where he stood at the top of the world.

Sam noticed Shaw's faraway look. "Tell me what you're thinking."

"It was them. Or at least one of them. The woman, I think. Karla Brigan."

"What?" Sam leaned forward. "Who? When?"

"Last week. Don't ask me what day. I stopped counting days months ago."

"You saw them?"

Shaw shook his head, explaining to Sam where he had been at dusk when he heard what he now knew was a woman's scream. What he failed to tell Sam was that he now believed it was a *dying* scream. A scream that you don't come back from, thrown out in a last, desperate hope that someone will hear it and will know where to find your body so your loved ones can grieve.

And he had heard it. If it was Karla Brigan—she was certainly dead.

"Let's go find them," Shaw said, facing Sam, a glint of excitement in his eyes. "I know where to look." Like the sound of the scream, Shaw had also committed to memory an estimate of the location of the sound. It was rough at best, yet it was a start at least.

"What?" Sam said as though Shaw was suggesting the unthinkable.

"Sam, you know the area. You've got Ghost plus a ton of experience in search and rescue. Why not?"

"Because it could take months," Sam argued. "I don't have the resources to stage such an ongoing search."

"Then let's just take a look." Shaw was persistent now. He felt somehow responsible for not acting when he first heard the scream. "Just for a few days. We'll go hiking. Take a tent, some supplies. You can show me some of the natural beauty of the place."

"All the while looking for a missing couple?"

"Isn't that what you do?" Shaw asked, realizing the statement had a subtle double meaning to it. Sam Rubino had spent most of her life searching for her mother. Every day, venturing into the wilderness, holding on to what may be, indeed, a lost cause. Sam thought it over. Maybe it would be good to get out of the cabin, take a trip up into the mountains for a few days.

Shaw touched her knee. "Come on. It will be good. Plus I want to know what happened to this missing couple."

Sam gave him a long, hard look before saying, "I only have a small tent."

Shaw gave a slight smile. "We'll improvise."

So for the rest of the evening, they planned their impromptu trip into the unknown. Sam pulled out an old ordnance map she had kept of the area, asking Shaw to, as best he could, pinpoint where he thought the sound had emanated from. Looking at the map, Sam knew it was no easy task. "Let me make it really clear from the get-go," she warned Shaw.

He looked up from the map.

"There is next to no chance we're going to find anything. I've got nothing of theirs for Ghost to possibly track a scent with. Nothing."

Shaw thought about it for a moment and then gave Sam a sly smile.

"No," she insisted, suddenly understanding.

Shaw gave her an innocent look.

"No," Sam repeated, louder and firmer this time.

He brought her some food and bottled water but didn't undo the restraints at all.

Bridget McKenzie's feet were bound, and steel manacles were snapped around her wrists, which were attached to a heavy chain that clinked every time she moved. She wore a full latex rubber hood with holes just for her nose and mouth. It was secured in place with a heavy strap and padlocked buckle at the base of her skull. She had used her fingers as best she could to claw at the mask, trying to pry under the seams or at the strap that was wrapped around her throat. But it held firm. She was blind; however, her fingers had become her eyes, to grope, feel, and touch her way along the floor of her prison. As she explored, listened for the slightest sound, noted particular smells, judged direction and distance, a mental construct of her surroundings began to form inside her pitch-black mind.

The floor was bone cold, dusty cement, and the smell of diesel hung in the listless air. There was no draft, and no light that she could tell. She tried to jump, see if should could reach something above her head, but empty air was all she grasped. She beat the chain on the ground, listened as the heavy echo vibrated in the cavernous space. There was a door, steel and heavy, somewhere above her, to her right. She had pinpointed its location when she had sat directly under the ring in the wall where the chain was attached. She could hear the scrape of metal, the rattle of a lock, dry hinges creaking when he entered. There were stairs, too, which vibrated with the sound of heavy feet on metal as he descended toward her.

The fact that the mask she wore had no gag was cold comfort for Bridget. It meant she was someplace isolated, well away from curious ears and prying eyes. No matter how loud she was, her screams would go unnoticed.

And when he came, three times now, he said nothing. Just nudged her with the toe of his boot, pressed the water bottle into her hand. She drank the water greedily and then asked a barrage of questions that went unanswered. Her pleas soon became curses as she swore at him. Bridget was not one to fold, to cave in, and beg for her life. She was a fighter, always had been. He would crouch down in front of her every time. She could feel him there, sense his eyes on her, over her body. He was inert though. No scent whatsoever. No bad breath. No stink of sweat. No reek of aftershave. Nothing.

After the water, he would place a plastic bowl on her lap, some sloppy muck out of a tin with a plastic spoon to feed with. She only ate because she needed to keep her strength up, not wane into a weak, groveling mess. That would play right into his plans, she imagined. She was going to wait, choose the right moment.

However, as she lay on the floor, in those lonely stretches, something did give her cause for alarm.

Toilet facilities. There were none. He hadn't gestured her toward anything, and as far as she could tell from her limited exploration on her hands and knees, her fingers hadn't discovered a bucket of any kind either. Mind you, the chain she was tethered to was short, only allowing her to search a few feet in front of her, and apart from the solid wall at her back, Bridget hadn't been able to reach the other three walls or any other objects in the room.

It must be a basement she was in. And the fact that he had no concern for her bodily functions only meant one thing.

Something bad was going to happen to her—soon.

# Chapter 24

There was nothing quite like the feeling of a country fair at the end of summer.

The sweet smell of cotton candy and freshly baked apple pies. Of toffee apples and deep-fried chicken. With the end of fall would come winter, the snow season, and the mountain would be inundated with skiers and winter tourists in the coming months. But until then, the air still held the last of the summer warmth, with a cooler edge to it. The sky was a deep indigo, flickering with bright flashing colors from the fairground rides and filled with the sound of fearful but excited screams.

Sam moved through the tide, Shaw by her side. Between the food stalls, he caught a glimpse of a swing ride, shrieks and shrills flung off into the dusk air as it sped around.

It had taken a supreme effort for Sam to convince Shaw to come along to the fair. It was one of the few annual attractions in Bright Water that drew in the entire town and most of the population from the region. Shaw had listened to Sam patiently as she pleaded her case. She didn't want to go alone. They would only stay for an hour at most. Two hours later, they were still there, sampling food and wandering between the rides, food stalls, and agricultural displays.

Taking Shaw's arm, Sam spied something and steered him down an adjacent alley. Moments later Shaw found himself standing in front of a shooting gallery, a row of paint-chipped metal ducks sliding past on a rickety conveyor, shelves crammed full with plush toys, a row of eager kids, and determined adults hunkered down on a worn wooden counter that ran the length of the front, small air rifles in their hands.

Delivering his well-rehearsed spiel, the attendant waved and coaxed the passersby, urging them to step right up and win a prize. "Everyone gets a prize!" he sang at the top of his voice. The top shelf was where the best prizes sat undisturbed. Huge soft elephants, unicorns, bears, and lions, tempting the gullible.

"Did I tell you how good a shot I am?" Sam said, gazing up at Shaw, with all the exuberance of a young child on Christmas morning. The lights from the surrounding rides glinted in her emerald eyes, her hair glowing like bright, fiery copper.

"No, you didn't," Shaw replied. "Why do I think you're about to give me a demonstration?"

Sam smiled gleefully. She hadn't felt this good in ages, and it was all due to the man who now stood next to her. She had been hidden away for too long in her cabin, preoccupied all these years. She needed a break, have some fun before she forgot entirely how to have fun.

A spot opened up at the counter, and quickly Sam squeezed in between a serious-faced man who was trying desperately to impress his wife or date, and a gangly teenager who seemed more interested in shooting everything but the metal ducks as they slid past.

Without warning, for some subliminal reason, Shaw felt the urge to turn away, look behind him, past the rows of stalls and rides and through the weaving flow of people.

Roy Beckman.

He was standing—more like leaning—in an overly confident slouch against a steel barrier next to one of the fairground rides. One thumb hooked into his belt, his sheriff's hat pushed back on his forehead, a wide smile on his animated face. His posture was a complete contrast to when Shaw had last encountered him. The subject of Roy's overt and somewhat theatrical attention were two young women, perhaps no older than sixteen, dressed in skinny cut-off shorts and clinging tops. The two young women seemed beguiled by whatever Roy was saying to them. Plenty of giggling and hair twirling. It seemed innocent enough. And yet as Shaw continued watching, there was something disturbing about Roy's manner. It seemed forced, like he was trying too hard to impress. And the way he occasionally licked his lips, almost predatorily, sizing up a quick meal that was within his reach.

As though sensing someone was watching him, the smile faded from Roy's face. His expression tightened, he stood a little straighter, broke off from the conversation with the two young women, and swiveled his head toward Shaw's direction.

Shaw quickly turned back to Sam and said some words of encouragement.

Holding the rifle, Sam took steady aim.

Shaw glanced back over his shoulder to where Roy was standing, but he and the two women were gone. Shaw scanned the crowd but couldn't pick him out again.

The rifle held a ten-shot clip, and Shaw watched as Sam squeezed off all ten pellets, hitting only two of the ducks, knocking them down off their hinges. He gave a slight smile. She was a good shot but had failed to adjust her aim to compensate for the deliberate ploy.

Sam frowned, perplexed as to why she had missed. Then standing up from the counter, she shrugged. "Maybe my aim is off."

"Maybe," Shaw said, slipping smoothly into Sam's seat at the counter before holding up a five-dollar bill and beckoning to the eager vendor.

"You want to try your luck, sir?" the vendor said, smoothly and expertly taking the five-dollar bill from Shaw's raised hand and slipping it into his striped waistcoat.

Luck had nothing to do with it.

Shaw examined the air rifle and then took aim at one of the moving steel ducks, tracking it with the front sight as it bobbed past.

He squeezed the trigger.

The shot went high, and to the left, missing the line of moving ducks by a good two inches.

Sam laughed behind him. "I think you're going to lose your money."

Undeterred, Shaw tucked in snug behind the rifle again. But this time, instead of aiming the front sight at the row of moving ducks, he compensated, lowering the barrel, as though he was aiming below the line of moving ducks and into the padded area beneath the conveyor belt.

He pulled the trigger in rapidly, taking out a complete row of nine ducks in succession.

People stopped shooting. Heads turned. Jaws dropped open. Eyes went wide.

"Wow, mister," said the gangly teenager with freckles and a faded Patriots ball cap on seated next to Shaw. "Where did you learn to shoot like that?"

The cocky smile vanished from the vendor. His eyes narrowed as he regarded Shaw with a thin, knowing smile.

Shaw placed the rifle casually onto the counter. "I'll take the bear on the top shelf," Shaw said, pointing to a huge bear with a droopy head.

Reluctantly, the vendor reached up to the top prize shelf.

"Not that one," Shaw called out. "The red one." Shaw turned

to see Sam staring, wide eyed, at him. Her mouth open, no words coming out.

"You want the red bear?" Shaw asked.

Dumbfounded, Sam barely nodded and then gave Shaw a wry, suspicious smile. "Red is my favorite color," she said, finding her voice again.

"Mine too." Shaw almost had to wrestle the fire-engine red bear from the vendor's steely grip before thrusting it into Sam's welcoming arms. She cuddled the huge plush bear, burying her face into its soft body, and began to walk away.

"Gotta make a living," the vendor said to Shaw, managing to smile and grumble the words out at the same time.

Shaw leaned in close to the man and out of earshot of everyone else. "From the adults. Not the kids. You can take the adults' money, but let the kids win."

The man, now red faced, nodded while forcing a smile.

"I'll be back to check on you," Shaw continued. "If I don't see half that top shelf gone in the next thirty minutes and in a few kids' hands, I'll sit down again and take it all."

Shaw took Sam's elbow and guided her away from the shooting gallery. In the distance, above the crowds and the tops of the stalls, he could see the illuminated spokes of the Ferris wheel slowly turning in the rapidly darkening sky. "Let's find a quiet place to talk."

# Chapter 25

Slipping ten dollars—five times what the ticket price was to ride—to the Ferris wheel attendant, meant they could ride for as long as they wanted.

Sam and Shaw climbed into one of the cars and pressed up to one another on the small vinyl bench seat before being carried aloft, the din of the fairground fading below their dangling feet. As they slowly rotated through the darkness, Sam moved even closer, lifting Shaw's arm with one hand and placing it over her shoulders, burrowing herself into his side. "Don't get any ideas," she said. "It's cold up here."

"You've got the bear for that."

Sam clutched the bear on her lap, its head flopping over the safety bar in front. "I know, but I've got you too."

They said nothing for a few minutes, enjoying the steady rise and fall, alternating between the still quietness at the top of the arc before descending again into the noisy throng of people below.

At the top of the ride, the whole fair spread out below them. Grids of light fanned out in all directions, a sea of heads moving and flowing, faster at the edges, bottlenecked at the center. Occasionally, a shout or a scream, louder than the surrounding noise, would drift up toward them. To the east, the lights of the township of Bright Water twinkled, with the jagged silhouette of the mountains encircling it. The car swung back down, the sounds and smells intensifying, before slowly fading as the car was carried aloft again.

"So how come you can shoot like that?" Sam finally spoke, moving her hand onto Shaw's thigh, pulling the bear tighter with the other.

There was no subtle way to say it, so Shaw just came out with it. "I was in the US Secret Service."

Sam suddenly looked up at Shaw, her face just inches from his. "You're in the Secret Service?"

"Was," Shaw corrected her. "I resigned more than a year ago."

"Resigned? Why?"

"I'd had enough. Too much politics. I didn't like the games people were playing in Washington. Plenty of backstabbing and egos to stroke."

"So what happened?" Sam asked, knowing there was more to the story. You don't just *leave* the US Secret Service.

"Just stuff." Shaw didn't offer more.

Sam found this fascinating. He was young, good looking, and used to work for one of the most mysterious organizations on the planet. "Did you ever protect the president?" Sam asked, almost jokingly. Presidential protection, while being the most publicly visible function of the US Secret Service, in reality was only one role the agency was responsible for. The truth was, behind the secretive façade, the majority of agency staff were employed in investigating financial-based crimes such as counterfeiting, cybercrime, bank fraud, and identity theft. Only a small and very select group of agents were ever chosen to be in the exclusive protection detail charged with keeping safe the leader of the free world.

"Vice president," Shaw replied. It was no big deal to him.

Sam almost choked. "You're kidding me?"

Shaw shook his head.

"My God, I had no idea. I'm impressed."

"Don't be. The bulk of the work and credit should go to the agents who you never really see, the ones behind the scenes, the ones who follow up on all the threats, no matter how small."

"How many crackpot threats do you guys get?" she asked.

"Thousands each year. Some are serious, most aren't, but each one must be followed up on. Thousands and thousands of man-hours are spent doing background checks, looking into people's pasts. It's the agents who do all the tedious desk work like poring over reports and offender records, who should get the credit. Don't get me wrong, it's an honor to serve and protect a president or vice president, but the real credit should go to all those people behind the scenes. Ninety percent of work is data analysis. Like most agency work."

Sam smiled, amazed at the man she was practically sitting on top of now, unaware that during the conversation she was absentmindedly drumming her fingers on his thigh, wondering about the things he must have seen and heard behind the closed doors of the White House. "You still haven't told me what really happened. Why you resigned. There must be more to it than the backstabbing politics. That goes with the town."

Shaw remained silent.

"Do you have to kill me if you tell me?" Sam said teasing.

"It's a long story. I don't want to bore you with it. The short, unofficial version is that I was kicked out."

"Kicked out? Really?" She admired his honesty. She was truly captivated now.

Shaw decided to tell her. There was something about her he liked. He felt comfortable in her presence. His gut was telling him he could trust her. He looked directly into her eyes, his face suddenly serious. "This conversation is just between you and me. No one else."

"Deal." Sam held out her hand. Shaw shook it.

"I hit someone," Shaw said slowly, thinking back to that fateful night in Oklahoma City, in the hotel corridor, where he and another agent stood guard outside the vice president's suite. For twenty minutes they had heard the screams and cries come from within the room, on the other side of the locked door. They were both given strict instructions not to enter the room, no matter what they heard unless the vice president hit his panic button or called out to them.

"You hit the vice president? The current one? The senator from Idaho? I've never liked him. He has beady eyes and a face I just don't trust."

Shaw smiled. He liked her even more. "Yes, I hit him. Punched him in the mouth."

Sam went wide eyed, totally engrossed. "Why? What did he do for you to punch him?"

Shaw never regretted what he had done. He had always stayed true to himself. That was important to him. While the world lately seemed to ebb and flow between moral hypocrisy, self-gratification, and oversensitivity, Shaw always grounded himself on truth, honesty, and speaking and acting out one's mind—no matter what the consequences.

"What he was 'doing,' as you put it, was a fourteen-year-old girl in his hotel room, while his wife and children slept peacefully fourteen hundred miles away in Boise, Idaho."

Roy Beckman stood in the shadows watching them walk across the makeshift parking lot that had been set up on a grassy field.

What intrigued him the most, apart from the fact that he didn't expect to see Sam there, was the man she was with again.

The same man he had seen before at her cabin, and who had also been in his barn with Sam, poking around. As much as he had tried to find him again, Roy hadn't seen the man around town—and he made it his business to know everyone in town, resident or visitor alike. He didn't want to ask Sam about her new companion either. That would be a sign of weakness, like he was going to her for help.

Roy didn't like the way the man kept popping up. However, in a strange way, he was glad Sam was with someone else. Not that her happiness or well-being mattered to him. Quite the opposite. In his mind, Sam Rubino's happiness was entirely dependent on him. He knew, deep down, he could bring her enduring happiness—or total misery. Which one ... was entirely up to her.

The appearance of the stranger presented Roy with a test, a challenge. Something that would give him focus, purpose, another angle of intervention, other than what he had been doing recently.

Roy watched from the shadows as Sam tossed the stranger her car keys. He caught them one handed in the darkness, revealing a glimmer of the man's inner workings.

Confident. Self-assured.

Seeing this angered Roy even more as he continued to watch. She had never allowed him to drive her precious SUV. British piece of junk it was anyway. Perhaps the man was a threat, after all, someone to contend with. Tony Lombardi seemed to think so.

Sam's SUV swung out, forcing Roy to duck behind the tall side of a large pickup truck, just as the headlights swept over where he was standing seconds ago. The SUV slid past before pulling out onto the main road and heading toward town. Roy stood up and watched for a moment in the cold darkness, his shimmering outline framed by the aura of the fairground lights behind him.

Finally the red taillights of Sam's SUV faded to nothing, and Roy trudged back to his own vehicle, nothing but malicious intentions swirling in his head.

He had work to do.

# Chapter 26

Sam offered him the sofa, said it was fine if he wanted to stay the night and return to his own place in the morning.

It wasn't that late, but Shaw preferred to get going, walk back through the woods to his own cabin. He knew the way even in the dark.

Trying to hide her disappointment, Sam put on the coffeemaker, convincing Shaw to stay just for one cup.

She stoked the fire and disappeared into the galley kitchen while Shaw sat on the sofa, Ghost on the mat at the back door.

Sam came back with two cups of coffee.

"Were you telling the truth when you said red was your favorite color?" Sam asked, eyeing Shaw over the rim of her coffee cup.

Orange was Shaw's favorite color. Close enough to red. "Yes, I was."

Sam watched him carefully. "What about redheads?"

Shaw shrugged deliberately.

Sam placed her coffee cup on the table. "Is it the freckles?" she asked, slightly dejected at Shaw's tepid responsiveness. Her eyes searched the floor, the night not going as she had hoped. "I think I have too many." Sam's voice was almost a whisper as though she was talking to herself. She didn't like the freckles on her face, made her look juvenile.

She looked up suddenly, expecting Shaw to disagree, but he said nothing, seemed more engrossed in watching the flames in the fire than paying attention to her, his mind preoccupied.

Moments passed without a word between them, leaving Sam thinking that this was a bad idea. "I hate how I look," Sam finally said in a scolding tone.

"I like how you look." Shaw's eyes were still watching the flames dance and flicker in the fire. "And I like your freckles too." Finally he looked at her. "Come closer."

For a moment, Sam just stared at him unsure of what had he just said.

"Closer?"

Shaw nodded.

"Why?" She stood but didn't move.

Shaw's face was expressionless. No smile. No frown. Just blank. And yet Sam found it extremely suggestive, like he was testing her to take a step forward, to cross the line that would change everything between them.

"Why come closer?" Sam repeated defiantly. He had been rude, ignoring her. Why should she take the first step? He should come to her.

Blank faced, Shaw replied, "So I can count them on your face."

Those words were enough. Any inhibition or annoyance Sam felt evaporated. Tentatively, Sam stepped forward until she was standing directly in front of him, their knees touching, Sam standing, Shaw seated on the sofa.

He looked up at her, and without breaking his gaze, slid both his hands slowly up and behind her calves, before working them up to the soft, sensitive flesh behind her knees, all the time watching Sam's reaction, never taking his eyes from hers.

Sam looked down at him, trying to read his face, keeping her own face emotionless, despite the pain of restraint she now felt. *Two could play at the game,* she thought. A battle of wills. Who would break first?

His hands slid farther up—and the line was crossed, the intent made clear by an extra two inches his hands traveled. Sam broke his gaze, closed her eyes, and saw the next two hours unfolding clearly in her mind.

With her eyes still closed, she could feel the fabric of her dress rise over her buttocks, and gather at the base of her spine, imagining his face precariously close to her most intimate domain. She inhaled deeply as his hands, firm but gentle, wrapped around her cheeks, drawing her closer to him.

She held her breath, her body trembling now.

She felt fingers hook under the elastic top of her panties, drawing them down in one smooth motion, over her buttocks, then down past her knees and to her ankles.

Sam didn't flinch. With her eyes still closed, she kicked them free.

She felt the front of her dress lift above her abdomen and bunch just above her belly button. She opened her eyes and gazed straight ahead, visualizing through the wall, out past the stream at the back of the cabin, and through the dark trees in the forest beyond.

Then he kissed her, delicate touches on her soft, fiery curls. They were well-placed kisses, considerate, mindful of her sensitivity.

Still looking in the distance at a vision only Sam could see, she stepped, her feet slightly apart, and pulled the back of Shaw's head closer to her, lower, angling his mouth down, then under, and finally upward and into her.

Then he *really* kissed her, his mouth molding perfectly into her inner reaches.

In her vision, Sam flew even farther and faster, breaking through the forest on the other side, shooting upward, before skimming the vaulted cliff tops and soaring even higher toward heaven itself.

# Chapter 27

Looking over her shoulder at her reflection in the mirror, she could see the first signs of the bruises beginning to emerge through her skin up near her shoulder blades. Small, dark finger-mark blemishes.

Nothing too serious. Just enough to give her some cause for concern. Sam knew he wasn't a violent person, not in that way, at least. However, there was something there, lurking in *his* darkness, something she had caught a glimpse of, when the fabric of his release finally tore through him. Something else had come out, revealing itself to her. Nothing evil, though, she didn't think—she hoped. But it was something disturbing, the stuff of nightmares—the same kinds nightmares she'd had herself.

It had left her thinking, as she lay awake long after he had gone still next to her, both of them wrapped in the mayhem of sheets and blankets. Like her, he had seen something, experienced something that had left a permanent taint on him as sure and as difficult to remove as a tattoo.

Sam had seen the detritus, what gets left behind when pure evil had its way. And yet in all these years, she had never seen, face-to-face, the perpetrator of the acts she had the displeasure to locate the aftermath of. That was left for the police to do.

Perhaps Shaw had experienced both: the aftermath as well as the perpetrator of something truly bad that had left him damaged. We were all damaged goods in one way or another. Whether we chose to show such damage was a matter of individual choice.

And he would never harm her. But something or someone had harmed him.

He wasn't a bad person. Far from it. In that pinnacle moment, when he hunched and twisted and convulsed in what seemed like pleasure that soon descended into pain, it was as much as she could do to just hold on while the freight train careened along the track before smashing into the barrier at the end of the track and coming to an abrupt halt. Sam would check the brackets of the bed later, certain they would need tightening, realigning from what had transpired last night.

Sam checked her skin one more time but couldn't find any others. She quickly got dressed, towel dried her hair, and found Shaw sitting at the small table on the back porch, drinking coffee and watching the morning sun creep above the treetops.

He smiled at Sam when she sat down next to him. "I'm sorry if I frightened you," he said.

"You didn't frighten me. Far from it." Last night had taken her into the heights of euphoric delirium that she never knew existed. But what she did know was that it would take a few days for her to come down from that lofty perch he had placed her on.

They said nothing for a few minutes, content to just watch the forest move, the stream flow, the blades of sunlight ripple and glow. In the distance, on the other side of the bank, Ghost rummaged, snout down, through the undergrowth. Occasionally he would lift his head, throw a look in Sam's direction to make sure she was safe before resuming his foraging.

"Have you thought anymore about heading up into the mountains?" Shaw asked, not wanting to discuss last night any further.

"I have," Sam replied.

"And?"

She turned to Shaw, studying his face. He certainly was an enigma. One that she intended to take the time to decipher.

"I will need to make some preparations. Check in on my father too. Make sure he is okay."

Shaw wanted to say something but thought better not to meddle in family business.

"Tomorrow," Sam continued. "We will leave then. In the morning. At sun up. I just need to go into town today and buy a few provisions. You can come with me if you like."

Shaw nodded. "Just give me an hour to go back to my cabin. Have a shower. Get changed."

Sam agreed and said she would drop by and pick him up in an hour.

While Shaw was gone, and with Ghost still roaming the perimeter of the cabin, Sam went to the storage shed and dug out an old two-person tent and a hiking backpack, which she hadn't used in years. She dusted them both off, checked that everything was in order, then went back inside the cabin and made a list of provisions they would need. Sam intended to travel light, take Ghost as well. He could sleep outside the tent at night. It wasn't that cold, and the last time she remembered sharing a tent with him, he had hogged the tight space, sprawling out.

Shaw was standing on the side of the road at the top of the dirt track that led down to his cabin when Sam drove by. He had an earthy, fresh scent to him when he slid in next to her.

First, they visited the general store, purchased lightweight provisions, vacuum-sealed, dehydrated meals. No fuss, minimal mess. Sam wore a ball cap tightly over her flaming hair, which she had tucked up under the cap, methodically going about her business, not stopping to chat with townsfolk who greeted her in the street or came out of the store.

Next, they stopped for a brief bite to eat at a café, a local establishment renowned for tasty, Middle Eastern comfort food. Sitting next to the bay window, Sam seemed preoccupied with watching the passing traffic while Shaw admired the vibrant wall art.

"Three days," Sam said. "That's about the limit of what we can carry ourselves without getting loaded down."

"That should be enough. I don't expect to find them, but I'd like to take a look anyway."

Sam had already checked the weather forecast for the next seven days. It was the end of summer, so the temperature would be cool at night, but nothing compared to winter when the snow came, dragging the tourists along with it, and an avalanche of fancy electric SUVs that lined up for the only Tesla Supercharger, which was located across the street from where they were sitting. It stood unused for the rest of the year.

Sam had already spoken to Woody to get an update on the missing couple. Still no sign of them, and he had said the local police and sheriff's department were confident they had just got lost and soon would reemerge from the forest with no more than a few scratches and slight disorientation.

They left the café and drove to Sam's father's house. While Sam went inside, Shaw walked around the property. It was a simple one-story ranch-style house. The garden had once been cared for, planned out, tended to. Now it was reduced to a dirt patch of rambling weeds. The houses on both sides and across the street were built from the same era, with kept yards and regular maintenance. Shaw started at the front and slowly made his way backward, watching the angles and sight lines change with each step, taking in which windows from the surrounding houses had a clear view of Sam's father's house. Old habits by Shaw, trying to figure out who had perhaps seen Laura Rubino walk out the front door that fateful day thirteen years ago, never to return. Did she go on foot, alone, or was someone waiting for her? Did a neighbor see a car pull up and she got in? Was someone waiting for her in the shadows with evil intent? Was there a struggle? Or did Laura Rubino go of her own free will? Someone must have seen something. They always did. Whether or not they bothered to notice or just dismissed it as nothing out of the ordinary was another matter entirely.

The upstairs curtains of a neighbor's house moved, a shadow passing behind it. Shaw ignored it as he continued his walk, trying to form a mental picture of the house, the trees, the entire street thirteen years ago. The foliage would have been a little thinner. The house siding less faded. The surrounding houses a little less aged.

Sam came out the front door, saw Shaw across the street, and wondered what he was doing.

Just before Shaw climbed into her SUV, he glanced across the street one last time, up to the window where he had seen movement. There, standing in full view, the drapes drawn aside, stood a women, old, in her seventies perhaps. She was looking down into the street—directly at Shaw, a look of pity in her eyes.

# Chapter 28

On their way back through town, Sam decided to fill the Land Rover up with gas.

As they pulled into the gas station, something caught Shaw's attention across the street where a strip of stores were. "I'll be back," he said to Sam, who had the gas cap off and was pumping gas.

One particular store had Shaw's interest. A Closed sign hung from behind the glass. He tried the front door, just to make certain, but it was locked, and the windows were dark, no sign of activity inside. Shaw stood in front of the McKenzie store, looking at the Opening Hours sign in the window. The store should be open.

"Ain't been open since yesterday," a voice came from behind Shaw. He turned to see an old man standing there with gray hair, a wizened face, dressed in a plaid shirt and well-worn blue jeans. In one hand he carried a gas can. "Need some kerosene for my lamps." The man looked at Shaw. "But the place is shut."

"What about the gas station across the road?"

The old man scrunched his weathered face and shook his head as though Shaw had suggested he eat his own feces. "Total rip off, that place across the street." The man shuffled forward and gave a chuckle. "Saw what you did the other day with that axe of yours."

Shaw raised an eyebrow.

"That Joey Lombardi is a piece of work, just like his father. Deserved it, if you ask me. Been putting his squeeze on most businesses around here. Raising the rent for no apparent reason, then kicking people out when they cannot afford it."

"Is that right?" Shaw said.

The man pointed at the McKenzie store with the fuel can. "Been buying my kerosene near on fifty years from the McKenzies. Ain't gonna start buying it elsewhere."

Shaw glanced across the street. He couldn't see Sam, but her Land Rover was still parked at the pump. "Maybe it's not open today," Shaw suggested. "Day off."

The man scowled. "Ain't been closed in fifty years. That young lass in there usually opens it up like clockwork each morning." The old man wandered off cursing to himself.

Shaw glanced across the street and noticed that a sheriff's cruiser that had pulled into the gas station, was parked right across the front of Sam's SUV, blocking it in. Roy Beckman climbed out just as Sam was walking out of the gas station, carrying two take-out coffees.

Shaw let out a sigh and started over. He didn't want to confront Roy Beckman again and was certain Sam didn't want to either.

Out of nowhere, a black, jacked-up pickup truck pulled up tight to the curb and skidded to a halt, blocking Shaw's path. The pickup truck was so huge it blocked Shaw's view of the gas station. Four doors flew open, and out piled Joey Lombardi and three hefty-looking men. Joey locked eyes on Shaw and headed toward him, like a shark homing in on a school of bait fish.

Shaw stepped back but kept his hands by his sides.

"Hey, fucker!" Joey snarled, pointing a finger at Shaw as he strode forward, venom in his eyes, his face twisted like a Halloween mask. "Where do you think you're going?" Joey had been circling the town with some of his father's hired help from the ski resort. The three men were big, burly ski lift mechanics, used to lifting heavy steel and hauling chains and gears. During the off-season, they acted as additional security for the Lombardi family as Joey went around harassing business owners for unpaid rent and serving notices to vacate. Lately, they had been corralled into an eviction squad, kicking out tenants and throwing them and their possessions out onto the street.

Joey looked up at the store that Shaw was standing in front of. "Ah, isn't this nice." He smiled at Shaw like a hyena. "After a piece of sweet ass, are we?" Behind Joey, the three goons had bunched up, thick arms across their even thicker chests, thick-lipped smiles on their squashed, Paleolithic faces. Shaw's eyes took in each of the three goons before finally settling on Joey Lombardi. A lot of brawn, little brain, and plenty of explosive, fast-twitch muscle fibers that would tire easily.

"You hacked my car with your axe," Joey spat. "What the hell, man!"

Shaw let out a bored, deep sigh. He wasn't denying it. Yet he wasn't going to admit to it either. Shaw sidestepped, trying to go around Joey and his posse, but the three goons mirrored his movement, fanning out and blocking his path.

"Hold it, asshole," one of the goons said. "You ain't going nowhere."

Joey stepped back, preferring not to get any blood on his new Burberry polo shirt. "It's retribution time. And I want payback in pain and suffering."

Shaw looked questioningly at Joey. "Really? Do we have to do this right now?"

Joey grinned, revealing a row of sharp, perfectly formed, white teeth courtesy of some Bentley-driving cosmetic dentist in Manhattan. "The door cost five grand to fix," Joey said begrudgingly, jutting his chin out at Shaw. "You're going to need five times as much as that in dental work alone by the time we have finished with you."

"We?" Shaw gave a puzzled look. "There is no 'we.' All I see is three apes with tiny dicks and a man-child with a vagina."

Joey bunched his fists in rage. One of the goons—the one on Shaw's right—shuffled forward, a snarl across his face. Shaw halted him with a raised palm. "Not here. Not in the street. There are women and children around. They might get frightened."

Joey swiveled his head, looking around. The footpath was deserted on this side of the street. He frowned at Shaw.

Shaw pointed his finger at each of them in turn, the goons first, and counted off. "One, two, three women." Then he pointed at Joey last. "And one child."

But before Joey could respond with more abuse, Shaw said with a jerk of his thumb behind him. "Out back. In the alleyway." Without waiting for a response, Shaw turned his back on Joey and his entourage and began walking down the alley between the buildings.

About halfway into the alley, there was a blue steel dumpster on Shaw's left that reeked of putrid food waste, and in the air above the closed steel lid, a buzzing black cloud hovered. The ground was puddled with dirt and broken cement, that offered enough crunching sound for Shaw to know without turning to look, that all four of them were following—and exactly how they were following, in a line, stacked up like on a conveyor belt. Shaw sped up, almost into a jog, as though he was making a run for it.

The crunching footsteps behind him sped up too.

Good.

Shaw spun around, reversed direction, and ran at the first goon in the line, pushing off the ground, getting airborne with a flying knee that any Muay Thai fighter would have been proud of.

The first goon in line, who was still jogging forward, was caught by surprise as Shaw's knee crashed into his face, smashing his nose and spreading it across his face. Shaw was on to the next goon even before the first one had collapsed, planting his face into an oily, dirty puddle. Just like the first goon, the second was taken by surprise too. He saw the head of his comrade in front whiplash back violently before the man went down face-first into the dirt.

Shaw planted one foot, immediately pivoted on the ball of his foot, and swung low and hard with his other leg, the same leg he had dispatched the first goon with, catching the second goon's ankle joint with the instep of his foot in a brutal, bone-separating sweeping kick. The result was instant. The bone separated, and the man's foot skewed sideways, at a near right angle to his leg. He screamed and hopped onto his other leg, lifting his deformed leg off the ground. Shaw could have moved on to the next goon, victim number three. But he didn't. Something unleashed deep inside him. Flashes of images from the past flooded his mind: A dark underground chamber where he had nearly drowned. The deranged smile of the psychopathic misogynist, Dylan Cobb, cattle whip in one hand, a brain-sectioning knife in the other. Cold ashes in the fireplace of an empty beach house by the sea, hidden among the dunes and beach grass. The sound of crashing waves, and the face of a woman he couldn't save.

Waves of desire came crashing down on Shaw. Desire to destroy everything in front of him.

He switched his stance, pivoted back, and swept the other

ankle, breaking it this time, taking it out completely from under the second goon, laying him horizontally in midair for a millisecond before he came crashing to the ground in a screaming heap. Both his feet crippled and crooked.

The third goon, the last of the gang, however, had enough time to react. Seeing his first comrade go down, he quickly sidestepped the second man in front of him before Shaw cut him down with two vicious ankle kicks. The third man slipped on brass knuckles over one meaty hand. But these were no ordinary implements of bone-fracturing pain and damage. These were handcrafted, fashioned by him in his own workshop. Lovingly cast from a special blend of molten carbon steel that train tracks were made from. While still hot and malleable, the steel had been hand forged, shaped into an ugly skeletal glove with conical spikes across the top, the outer edges machine polished to a razor finish.

He had bloodied the cruel implement on a number of unsuspecting victims, inflicting horrendous injuries and permanent disfigurations that no amount of reconstructive surgery could fix. They had also been proudly used to deliver one-punch killing blows to others, where skulls were lethally fractured.

And that's what the man wielding the brass knuckles intended to do right now as he slowly circled Shaw—to smash his skull to smithereens.

# Chapter 29

*Crap.*

Sam stopped walking. Roy Beckman was casually leaning against the hood of her vehicle. "What do you want, Roy?" Sam walked around him, opened the door, and deposited the take-out cups into the center console. Through the windshield she could see the smug look on Roy's face as he watched her lean over. She stepped back out and confronted him. "Shift your car. I'm in a hurry."

"Where you going?" Roy made no attempt to move; in fact, he slouched a little lower on the hood and tilted back his sheriff's hat, like he had all day. "Got another date with that guy I've seen you with?"

"You always were the jealous type, Roy," Sam countered. Glancing across the street, Sam couldn't see where Shaw had gotten to. There was a huge pickup truck parked awkwardly outside the row of stores, almost up on the curb. Not that she needed Shaw right now. She could handle Roy herself. She just wanted to get out of town and back to her cabin. She turned her attention back to Roy. "He's a good friend."

"So what's his name? This 'good friend' of yours." Roy was taunting her now and she knew it. But she wasn't going to give him the pleasure. It must be burning him up inside to know who Ben was. Tough luck. She wasn't telling him a thing.

"And where does he come from?" Roy added, straightening himself a little, almost reaching for his notebook.

"Why? So you can run him out of town, like you have done

145

to anyone I've shown the slightest interest in?" Instead of backing off, Sam stepped up to the plate, closer to Roy, looked him in the eye. "Does it make you hard?" she whispered, her voice soft and sultry. "Watching me all the time. I see you. I know you're there." Sam edged a little closer. "You can't have me, but he can—has already, and can have me any time he wants."

Roy's face stiffened.

Sam didn't stop, could feel the flush of adrenaline build inside her. She was tempted to mention the red backpack Shaw had found in Roy's barn, along with Martin Fassen's wallet, driver's license, and clothes. But she thought better of it. Shaw wouldn't be happy. They had discussed other plans they had, and they didn't want anyone finding out—yet.

"How's your drunk of a father?" Roy straightened up off the hood of the car, his shadow falling over Sam. She stood her ground, held his questioning gaze.

"Still sulking because your whoring mother left you both?"

In a heartbeat, her adrenaline boiled into anger.

Sam bunched her fists, then lashed out in fury at Roy's face.

"Kill him!" Joey Lombardi squealed, enjoying the spectacle of watching one of his men, the biggest, the most vicious, the last one standing, closing in on Shaw.

The third goon slowly circled, hunkering down, cannonball shoulders rotating slowly, loosening himself up. His extended arms were like oak trunks: bulging, knotted vascular slabs that pulsed as he moved, a massive curve of iron ringing one fist. His other hand was open, like a gargantuan grappling claw from a junkyard crane.

From the bulge at the front of the man's trousers, there was no doubt in Shaw's mind that the goon was enjoying this, relishing beating him to a pulp.

One of the goons, the cripple, slithered through the dirt and mud toward Shaw, pulling himself along with one arm, the other arm extended up, the hand grabbing at the air in a useless attempt to snatch at Shaw. Not wanting to get tangled up, Shaw stepped forward and quickly dispatched him for good with a ruthless head kick. The man didn't move again after that—ever. For Shaw, this was not the time to be considerate, to go easy. It was killing time. What mattered was getting out of the alley alive, deal with the consequences later.

Without moving his head, Shaw looked up. An old, cobweb-ridden security camera was perched high on one of the brick walls, and Shaw prayed it was working. Four on one. A better defense in front of a judge. Lethal force used to save his own life. Kill or be killed and all that crap.

The first goon was still facedown in the dirty puddle, no bubbles, no nothing.

"Kill him!" Joey screamed hysterically again, bloodlust in his eyes. "My dad will fix everything. Just kill him!" Like the coward he was, Joey hung back. Still close enough to witness the imminent pummeling of Shaw, hear the crack of cranial bones, and watch with morbid fascination Shaw's skull cave in, and feel the killing deep in his own gut, taste it in his mouth as though it was he who had done it with his own hands.

The goon lumbered forward, swung with his iron-encased fist, aiming at Shaw's head.

Roy Beckman caught Sam's fist, mid-flight, just inches from his face.

He held it there for a moment, gave an amused smirk. "Striking a sheriff will get you up to seven years in jail."

"I don't care," Sam hissed, trying to wrench her fist free. Roy's grip was viselike, and she was now regretting her reckless act.

"I could arrest you, you know. Throw you in jail."

"Then do it!" Sam's eyes burned with emerald wildfire. She hated Roy Beckman more now than ever and was certain both he and his father had been responsible all these years for spreading the rumors around town that her mother, Laura Rubino, had run off with another man.

Roy regarded her for a moment, contemplating whether or not to cuff her, have her thrown in jail for a few hours to cool off. She always was a temperamental one, prone to outbursts whenever her mother or father were mentioned. "Tell me his name, and where he lives in town, and I'll let you go."

"Get lost, Roy. I've done nothing wrong, neither has he. You can't just go around town arresting people." Sam looked at her hand enclosed in Roy's fist. "It must give you some pleasure assaulting a woman. My mother warned me about you, and your father!"

Roy looked visibly shocked, taken aback by Sam's comment, like he had just been slapped across the face. His face tightened, his eyes turned corpse-cold, his jaw muscles bunched. "What did you say about my father?" he growled through clenched teeth.

Sam saw something evil flood across Roy's eyes and tried to lean away from him. She glanced desperately around, saw a few people who hurriedly looked away, kept walking, heads down, not wanting to get involved. Sam glanced across the street toward where Shaw had gone, saw nothing. He had vanished. She turned back to Roy as he squeezed her hand harder. His face had morphed into a hideous rictus of a possessed person, like the devil had taken over his body.

Out of the corner of Sam's eye, just past Roy's shoulder, a flicker of darkness, a shape moving swiftly toward them. Roy Beckman buckled forward, releasing his grip on Sam's hand. He tumbled forward and only just managed to remain on his feet.

Turning and enraged, he saw Ben Shaw standing behind him, a smile on his face.

"Sorry," Shaw said. "Didn't mean to run into you. Must have tripped." Shaw walked past them, looked at Sam, and spoke like a disgruntled schoolteacher. "Sam, stop assaulting the sheriff." Shaw pointed up at several security cameras that hung from under the gas station awning. "They'll have footage of everything."

Shaw turned back to Roy, his smile even wider. "Isn't that right, Sheriff?"

Roy recovered and was seething with anger. He glanced up at the camera lenses that were pointing down at him. The look of anger slowly faded from Roy's face as he regarded Shaw. Two can play at this game. "I want to see some identification, pal."

Shaw gave a shrug. "Why?" He nodded toward the Land Rover. "I'm not behind the wheel. I'm not the one driving." He nodded at Sam. "She is."

Roy made a show of adjusting his belt, not happy that Shaw had a smirk across his face, almost challenging his authority. No one in this town challenged him. Before he could respond, Shaw raised his hands in submission, his demeanor nonthreatening, submissive, playing up to the array of security cameras overhead. "You can't compel me to identify myself without reasonable grounds that you believe I've done, or are about to do, something illegal."

Roy's hand went to his Taser on his hip—then halted. He

cocked his head, resisting the tremendous urge he felt to deploy the Taser and zap the man in front of him.

Sam glanced from Shaw to Roy, then back to Shaw, and felt warmth rush inside her. No one had ever fought in her corner, for her.

Roy hesitated and then withdrew his hand from the Taser.

Shaw stood his ground, hands dropping slightly. "Are we free to go, Sheriff?"

Reluctantly, Roy Beckman nodded.

"Good." Shaw dropped his hands, opened the door, and slid into the passenger seat. "Hot coffee!" He picked up one of the take-out cups from the center console. "Nice." Then took a sip, raising the cup toward Roy Beckman in a mock toast.

Sam gave Roy a self-satisfied stare, then climbed in and started the engine. She watched in the rearview mirror as they pulled away. Roy Beckman hadn't moved. He just stood there defiantly in the reflection.

Once they were clear of the town, Shaw's shoulders slumped and he tilted sideways, almost spilling the coffee, a painful grimace across his face. He had done well to maintain the charade of bright exuberance, ignoring the searing pain he now felt.

"What's wrong?" Sam said, a look of concern on her face.

He clutched at his side, his reply strained, his breath tight. "Nothing. I'll be fine."

Sam took her eyes off the road and looked at him. "No. Something is wrong!"

Shaw pointed through the windshield. "Just drive. Don't worry about me. I'll be fine."

Sam focused back on the road. "You look like you need to go to the ER." She pressed the gas pedal a little harder and the V8 responded with a growl.

"No!" Shaw replied. "I just need some rest."

Sam shook her head. "What happened back there? When you wandered off?"

Shaw adjusted himself in the seat, trying to get comfortable, finding a position that would ease the pain he felt in his ribs. "I went to the zoo," he replied with a painful grin.

"The zoo!" Sam exclaimed.

Shaw took a deep breath, then instantly regretted it. "I fell into the gorilla enclosure. Had to fight my way out."

In the hot, dark stench of the steel dumpster, Joey Lombardi's cries for help went unnoticed, just bounced and echoed off the rusty walls of the steel box.

His wrists were bound behind his back with his own trouser belt. He lay on his side in a sour, rancid slush of rotten food scraps, mixed with tepid meat and vegetable juice, sprinkled with festering maggots. A large leaf of brown Chinese cabbage—that had once been green—clung to the side of Joey's bloodied face, the head injury sustained when Shaw had opened the steel lid, then upended him inside, headfirst, before uttering the words, "taking out the trash," then promptly slamming the lid shut.

# Chapter 30

They swung by Shaw's cabin to collect his gear.

To say that he traveled light would have been an understatement. Sam glanced into the back seat, where he had thrown a simple backpack and jacket. She could tell by how he was moving that he was favoring his left side, the right side of his body compensating. His injury, or whatever it was in his rib area. She knew it was pointless to keep asking him about it. He had deflected all her concerns so far. So she changed the subject.

"What?" Shaw said, climbing in next to her, noticing the look on her face. "Nothing," Sam said innocently as she pulled away, a slight smile on her lips. "It's just that you don't seem to have much—" Sam paused, not wanting to sound offensive.

"Possessions?" Shaw said.

Sam made a face. "I wouldn't have chosen that particular word. It sounds too materialistic."

"That's because it is."

Sam wasn't materialistic at all. Most of her friends who had left the town and had started lives of their own seemed to be in a race as to who could accumulate the most pointless "stuff" before they died. She had given up long ago scrolling through their Facebook pages, each photo a carefully staged montage of excess. Each video a Spielberg-choreographed insight into self-interest and instant gratification. The same was with LinkedIn. If Sam got one more prompt to "congratulate" one of her ladder-climbing friends for being in a job for five years, she would vomit. Once, Sam had actually typed on someone's page,

*Congratulations for being in the same office cubical for twenty years! You poor bastard.* But then didn't have the courage to post the message.

The self-indulgent crap people posted on social media ... *Who cares how much discount you got off your tenth Kate Spade bag or the chef's knife your son brought you back from Japan with your name specially engraved on it. No—one—cares!*

In a way, Sam was glad she had remained in Bright Water. She was happy there, content, grounded living in *her* cabin in *her* woods, with *her* dog. It was pure joy to wake up each morning to the clear mountain air, the birds, the bubbling stream, and the raw, peaceful movement of nature around her—not the incessant wail of sirens and constant drone of pedestrians and cars. Her city friends can keep their soy lattes, fake nails, and Botox smiles.

It wasn't for Sam.

However, there was part of her that knew some day she would move away, leave the place. The town and the memories here were slowly wearing her down.

Sam did want to find someone, a man with whom she could settle down and have kids with. Thought she had, with Roy. That was until his true colors started to show through.

Arriving back at Sam's cabin, they promptly went about organizing their gear. Sam was surprised at how much gear actually did fit into Shaw's backpack.

It was late afternoon by the time they were finished.

"Your last hearty meal before it's dehydrated stew and trail mix for the next three days," Sam said as she prepared a pot of spaghetti sauce.

"The more carbs the better," Shaw said. Dinner would be another thirty minutes, so Shaw grabbed a well-chewed rubber bone and went outside, Ghost by his side, the dog's eyes transfixed on the toy in Shaw's hand.

After stepping over the rocks and across the stream, Shaw headed up the slope on the other side and into the trees, Ghost not leaving his side, urging Shaw to throw the toy, which he did, hard and high into the trees farther up the slope.

Ghost took off like a missile, in a flurry of hind feet, and kicked-up dirt and leaves. Moments later the dog came bounding back, dropped the toy at Shaw's feet, and stared up at him.

Every time Shaw went to pick it up to throw again, Ghost would quickly grab it in his teeth, then drop it again, teasing Shaw. This game went on back and forth until Shaw finally snatched up the rubber bone and hurled it as hard and as far as he could through a gap in the trees.

Ghost bounded off again, and Shaw watched the dog's fluffy tail disappear over a small rise farther up the slope.

Shaw continued his climb, then paused and turned back to admire the view. Looking back down the hillside, he could see Sam's cabin nestled among the trees, a lazy spiral of smoke curling skyward. The cabin below looked smaller, almost toylike.

The sun dipped below the treetops, and long shadows started to pull themselves down the slope, creeping slowly toward the sunlit stream below and Sam's cabin, which still glowed under the last rays of the day.

Shaw resumed his climb, enjoying the exertion, the burn in his legs, the fresh, cooling air in his lungs. The pain in his side seemed less. No ribs were broken, just some bruising from where he'd been struck in the side with the brass knuckles. He was lucky, it was a glancing blow, not full force, a sacrifice Shaw had to make in order to get inside the man's guard and crush his larynx with a single throat punch. The third goon had gone down pretty fast after that. Twitched, shook, and gurgled for a few seconds, then went still, dead eyes wide open, staring back at Shaw in disbelief.

He reached the small rise expecting to see Ghost bounding back toward him, but the dog was nowhere to be seen.

Shaw stopped and swiveled his head all around him.

The woods were still and silent.

Shaw looked in all directions.

Nothing.

The ground sloped away from Shaw into a small gully below that cut a groove left to right that was choked with leaves and fallen branches. The temperature dropped noticeably as Shaw made his way down and stood in the gully, his ankles buried in dry leaves.

He hadn't thrown the toy that far. It would have landed somewhere down there on the other side of the slope.

Yet Ghost—staying true to his name—had vanished. Shaw knew the dog would eventually turn up, probably was distracted by an animal, and went off chasing it, a more interesting alternative than the rubber bone.

Shaw called out the dog's name and then waited, listening to nothing but the wind rustling the branches above him.

It was getting darker by the minute, perhaps only a half hour of sunlight left in the day, Shaw estimated. The dog would find his own way home, knew the woods up there better than he and Sam, Shaw imagined.

Shaw turned to head back up the rise when he saw something move, in the distance, a flicker of color between the tree trunks to his right. Shaw took off in that direction, his pace quicker now. Reaching the spot, he looked around again.

Nothing.

It was a person; he was certain of it. Someone was up there as well, in the woods. It could have been a hiker, just walking along.

Shaw searched the area for a few minutes but found nothing. Ghost still hadn't appeared.

There was nothing he could do as he headed back. The dog would be fine.

Sam was setting the table when Shaw walked in.

She looked up expectantly, saw a look of worry on his face.

"I think I lost your dog."

Sam waved him off. "He often takes off in the woods without me. He'll turn up. He always does. Don't worry about it. He's trained to find people who are lost. Not get lost himself."

Shaw nodded. That was true.

Sam went back to the kitchen before calling out, "Dinner is ready. Take a seat."

Shaw was still concerned about Ghost as he washed his hands, then sat down at the table. One minute the dog was there, and then he was gone. No bark. Not a sound. It was like the woods had swallowed him up.

Sam came back carrying two heaping, steaming bowls of spaghetti pasta topped with a rich tomato sauce. "I hope you're hungry," she said, placing one bowl in front of Shaw. "Walking in the woods is the best thing for an appetite."

A scratching came from the back door.

"I told you he'd be back," Sam said, getting up, and going to the back door. "It's dinnertime for him as well." Sam opened the door, and Ghost sauntered in, tail wagging, and went straight to Shaw.

"Thought I'd lost you," Shaw said, scratching Ghost behind an ear. "Where's your toy?" Shaw said, noticing the dog wasn't carrying the toy in his mouth.

Sam frowned, noticing the same thing.

"Did you bury it somewhere?" Shaw asked. "I hate to tell you this, bud," Shaw continued stroking the dog, before leaning down and whispering into the dog's cocked ear. "It's not a real bone. It's just rubber."

"He would never bury it," Sam said, hands on hips, a puzzled look on her face. "It's his favorite toy." She then shrugged. "Come on," she said to Ghost, "let's get you fed too." Sam disappeared into the kitchen only to appear moments later carrying a bowl of dog food, then placing it on a mat near the back door.

Ghost left Shaw and wandered over to the bowl, gave it a sniff, then walked to the rug next to the fire and plonked down.

Sam frowned. "Strange," she said, looking at Ghost. The dog watched them both from the rug, head down between his paws, big dark eyes flicking between them.

"He usually wolfs down his dinner." Sam resumed eating. "He only gets fed once a day, and he usually looks forward to it."

Shaw stopped eating and glanced at the dog. "Maybe he's not hungry." Shaw didn't believe his own words, but it seemed like the right thing to say. The dog was eighty pounds of canine muscle and bone. He would eat like a bodybuilder after a competition.

Sam continued to eat, but Shaw could tell her mind was preoccupied with Ghost. "Maybe, he'll eat later."

Sam nodded. "Maybe."

# Chapter 31

They were gone by first light, having packed everything the night before.

By noon they had traveled deep into the valley, and Shaw estimated from the map Sam had brought with her that they should reach the area where he had estimated the proximity of the sound he had heard at dusk that evening.

But they could be miles off from the actual location. The sound of a woman's scream had echoed and then drifted away on the early evening air. And even if they did manage to arrive at the location, what would they expect to find? The German couple could have moved on or been separated. They could be anywhere by now. Shaw, however was determined. After scrutinizing the map for hours the previous evening, he was certain they were heading in the general direction.

Plus he had something special in his backpack that he hadn't told Sam about. It may come in handy later.

Lunch consisted of trail mix and Clif bars shared between them while sitting on a boulder at the edge of a stream that rippled and bubbled over moss-covered rocks before emptying into a deep pool. The air was cool and fresh, yet they were both wet with perspiration from the morning hike.

She had circled a spot on the map that she wanted them to reach and set up camp before it got too dark. Sam had set a rapid pace, which suited Shaw. He was mountain-fit from the daily workouts he had been doing. Sam had led the way, Shaw just off her shoulder while Ghost was free to roam, scout ahead, or drift behind. At times Ghost would disappear into thick foliage, and Shaw would ask Sam if they should stop and wait for him to appear again. Sam shook her head, telling Shaw that if anyone was going to get lost, it was them and not her dog.

It felt good, though, for Shaw to have Ghost along for the ride. If anyone was following them or was ahead of them, then Ghost was certain to raise the alarm. However, so far, the dog just scouted and returned only to venture out again farther and would remain away for longer and longer stretches of time.

By late afternoon they had reached the predetermined location to camp for the evening. It was a spot well chosen by Sam, a high patch of ground with a large flowing stream nearby. Leaving their backpacks behind, they made their way down to the cool, inviting waters. Sam stripped down to her bra and panties, while Shaw sat in the shallows just in his shorts. Ghost appeared out of the forest and bounded into the water. Shaw found a stick and threw it to him. After a while, Ghost lost interest in the stick and disappeared back into the forest on the opposite bank.

Sam floated on her stomach over to where Shaw was and then paused a few feet away from his dangling feet. Her legs were drifting out behind her in the lazy current. "It will be dark soon," she said. "We should head back and get the fire started." She gave Shaw a coy smile.

Shaw's eyes drifted along the length of her back, then to the two bare orbs of pale skin that bobbed up in the water. He glanced around, then saw her bra and panties laid out neatly on a nearby rock, baking dry on the radiated heat.

Sam pulled herself forward through the water with her hands until she reached Shaw, and then tugged one of his ankles. "Get your ass in here."

Later, with a small fire built, and water heating in a small portable pot, they sat cross-legged in front of the tent. Sam had given Ghost some dried food, and the dog ate feverishly before slumping down next to her, exhausted from the distance they had traveled. The darkening sky brought with it an evening chill, and Shaw threw more wood on the fire from the stockpile he had gathered.

The freeze-dried stew they ate straight from the pouch was surprisingly good, and their canteens had been replenished in the clear waters of the mountain stream.

Sam unfolded the map again, held a small flashlight in one hand as she sat next to Shaw. "We should reach the location by lunchtime tomorrow. Late morning if we increase the pace."

"So let's go hard and see how far we get."

They agreed to have an early night. The inside of the two-person tent was small but cozy. Ghost slept outside by the dying fire.

It was just after midnight when the dog started going berserk.

# Chapter 32

"What is it?"

Sam stood next to Shaw in the darkness outside the tent. "I don't know," he replied. "But there's something out there." Shaw didn't want to turn on the flashlight. Ghost was madly barking and growling at the wall of trees in front of them. The fire had died down to smoky ash and orange embers.

Sam called Ghost. The dog ignored her. "It's a person, not an animal," she whispered, her eyes trying to cut through the ghostly silhouette of trees. "An animal—unless it was a real threat—wouldn't get him so riled up."

Shaw edged forward, straining to see into the gloom. Suddenly, as if something in the darkness had thrown out a challenge to the dog, Ghost barreled forward a few feet, then dug his paws, plowing to a stop, his jaws snapping like an industrial wood chipper. If it was a person, like Sam had said, then why didn't they just come out? Shaw finally flipped on the flashlight and panned it into the trees.

Nothing.

"Stay here," he said to Sam before taking off into the darkness in the direction the dog was barking. Sam moved forward, grabbed Ghost by the collar, and held him next to her.

Among the trees, Shaw laid down the flashlight on a log and walked away from it, cutting a path sideways, circling around. If someone was out there, he wanted to find them, catch them, without them seeing him approach. His eyes adjusted, yet everything was a sea of dark verticals. Barefoot, he trod softly, slow, deliberate steps as he slowly worked his way around in a wide arc away from where they had camped. The forest was eerily silent. No insects or animal noises. The moon slid past overhead through ragged clouds, offering watery light at best.

Something moved to his right, and the veil of darkness slithered over itself. Shaw turned and squinted into the distance. His eyes readjusted, trying to separate layers of watery blacks and dark grays.

A shape, an outline, materialized from the background of vertical tree trunks. Someone was hunkered down, a vague blob, head and shoulders, maybe thirty feet away. Shaw wondered if they had seen him too. Slowly he stepped over a fallen log, keeping himself hidden as best he could behind the tree trunks. He edged closer—the shape exploded. A person leaped up, ran hard and fast away from Shaw.

Shaw stood his ground and watched as the person faded into the background, the crunch of footsteps trampling foliage gradually receding. There was no point in chasing them. Whoever it was, they didn't want to be discovered, their intent obviously unfriendly.

Shaw returned to the campsite where Sam and Ghost stood.

"Who was it?"

"No idea. Whoever it was, they took off like a scalded cat."

"But it was definitely a person?"

Shaw nodded. "A man, I'd say. Judging from what I could see of them and how they ran."

Sam seemed unsettled. "Why would they run?" It was a question to herself. But Shaw answered it.

"Maybe they were frightened of the dog," he said, looking down at Ghost. Ghost's eyes were looking past Shaw, back into the forest where he had emerged from moments ago. The dog gave a low, guttural growl, the hairs on the back of its neck bristled.

"They were sneaking into the camp," Sam said. "Maybe they had been watching us earlier while we sat around the fire, talking."

Shaw shook his head. "Then Ghost would have made a noise, smelled them, I guess."

Sam nodded. True.

"Whoever they are, they're gone now." Shaw made his way back to the tent.

"I can't go back to sleep after that," Sam replied. "What if they come back?"

Shaw sat just inside the tent opening. "They won't. Ghost will alert us if they do."

Shaw watched Sam as she stood there, rubbing her shoulders not because she was cold. He sighed, dusted off his bare feet, then tugged on his boots. "I'll stay up," he said, getting up. "You get some sleep."

"You don't mind?" Sam said.

"Not at all. Ghost and I can talk secret male stuff." He imagined she had seen the aftermath of other people's sick cruelty. Yet the dark, the unknown, probably frightened her more.

Sam let out a deep breath. The relief on her face was instant. She gave Shaw a grateful smile.

Shaw grabbed a few logs, threw them on the embers of the fire, and stirred them with his boot. Moments later the fire took hold, and flames leaped up again, casting a wide orange glowing bubble of warm light around them that reached the tree line.

Sam retreated back to the tent.

Shaw sat down on a log and used a stick to poke the embers

some more, throwing up a burst of bright cinders into the velvet blackness above.

Ghost, seemingly unconvinced, stood facing the tree line, his body rigid, nose twitching, teeth bared.

Shaw sat back and stared at the flames for a while, enjoying the heat on his face and chest. Reluctantly, Ghost returned and settled down next to Shaw, his eyes never leaving the exact spot where he was barking at before. Shaw scratched Ghost behind one ear, and the dog nuzzled into his hand, but his eyes were unmoved.

Whoever it was, one thing was for certain—they were following them. Shaw didn't know who or why. But he was determined to find out before this trip into the mountains was over.

Sam woke the next morning to find Shaw returning from the forest with Ghost trotting beside him.

He told her as soon as dawn broke, he had ventured back out into the forest to see if he could find any traces or clues of the person who had been watching them last night. But he had found nothing.

After a quick breakfast, they broke camp and set off again.

By late morning they had reached the designated location on the map. The forest had thinned, and the terrain was relatively flat. A line of mountains rose in the distance. They had entered the foothills.

The next hour was spent scouting around, looking for any signs that anyone had been through these parts. Just after midday, they stopped for a dry lunch of energy bars and trail mix, and discussed what they were going to do next. Ghost was off rambling among the trees while Sam and Shaw sat on a cluster of large rocks. The wilderness around them seemed empty, still, devoid of anyone else.

Their search had produced no results, no trace of the missing backpackers or anyone else. No trash, no signs of a camp, or ground markings that anyone had been here.

"We could be literally miles away from where they were," Sam said as she sat, eating a granola bar.

"Well, at least we're out in the fresh air," Shaw replied, looking around, enjoying the trek so far. Yet in the back of his mind, like Sam, he was thinking about the stranger in the dark who had visited them last night. Neither of them had spoken again about the person after they had set off this morning. But it seemed to hang in the air over them. An unsolved mystery.

Sam had slept the rest of the predawn hours peacefully, secure in knowing that Shaw and Ghost were just a few feet away from the tent if she needed them. The entire incident had spooked her, Shaw could tell. As they hiked to this spot, she was constantly looking over her shoulder and around into the woods, almost expecting to see the dark shape of someone standing among the trees, staring creepily at them. But Ghost hadn't barked once on the morning trek, which was a good sign.

Finally, Sam broached the subject. "So who do you think it was?" she asked.

Shaw had a theory, not as to the actual identity of the person, more as to why they were there, watching them, wanting to remain hidden, not be caught. Any normal person, a hiker who was lost would be relieved to have found them, to see their fire last night, and would have gladly walked into the camp. But this person was intentionally watching them, didn't want to be found. In Shaw's mind, it wasn't the German couple. It was someone else.

"Roy Beckman?" Shaw offered. It seemed logical. But they were miles from the town. Unless he had taken a few days off work and saddled up with hiking gear and food to follow them. But no one knew they were there. Sam hadn't told anyone about their plans, and Shaw certainly had no one to tell.

"He's not that adventurous," Sam replied. "And I told no one."

"Maybe it's a wild child who grew up in the woods. Was abandoned and now lives out here," Shaw said, trying to make light of the situation, despite knowing that someone else was definitely there. On one occasion, while walking behind Sam, he got the distinct feeling someone was behind them, hidden among the trees. He didn't tell Sam, not wanting to alarm her any more.

"Maybe," Sam uttered, not convinced.

"Are you certain no one knows we are here?"

Sam nodded. "If a search is going on for the couple, they definitely wouldn't be out looking for them at night. They would be searching during the day. Not once it was dark."

That made sense to Shaw. No one would be searching the woods for the missing couple at midnight.

"What now?" Sam asked, not wanting to spend another night out there. It would be different if she had her gun. But she had left it safely locked away back in her cabin.

Shaw thought for a moment and then unzipped his backpack at his feet. He pulled out a plastic bag. Inside was a crumpled T-shirt that looked soiled. There were smudges of dirt on the front and sweat stains. Shaw handed it to Sam. "Take your dog and do what you do best."

Sam took the bag and stared at it, turning it over in her hands. She glanced up at Shaw, a look of shock in her eyes. "You went back and took this?"

Shaw gave a sly smile.

"You went back to the Beckman barn and took this from the red backpack?"

"What I believe to be Martin Fassen's backpack." Shaw nodded to the plastic bag in Sam's hands. "I'm guessing that this piece of clothing belongs to Martin Fassen."

"Why would Roy Beckman have a backpack belonging to a missing German tourist?" Sam asked.

"More importantly," Shaw said, "why is Roy Beckman hiding it in his barn and hasn't told anyone yet?" Shaw watched as Sam's expression tightened.

"Is it good enough for Ghost to pick up a scent if Martin Fassen was here, around this area?"

Sam opened the bag and carefully removed the shirt, her face serious. "There's only one way to find out." She whistled, and moments later, Ghost came bounding in.

# Chapter 33

He didn't know where he was.

It was cold, though, but he didn't care.

He was hungry, but he didn't care.

He was in pain, a lot of pain. Some of it physical, plenty of it not.

The bleeding had stopped. Infection, however, was a concern, especially out here. He imagined tiny little microbes, hundreds of them, maybe even thousands, fighting for a spot on the wound, at the edge of the tear in the skin, festering, and feeding on the flesh.

At times he felt delirious, light headed, disorientated. He had no idea where the car was parked. But it felt like it was miles away at the start of the trail. With the trees and foliage looking all the same to him, like a hall of mirrors, he couldn't even tell if he had covered the ground previously or not. Maybe he was going in circles. He didn't know.

He had washed the wound on his arm in a stream, gritting his teeth as he did, the frigid water coloring red for a moment. Shivering and cringing, waist deep, he'd watched as his blood cells were carried away by the ice-cold liquid. A little part of him would probably wash up in the mud and grit of the shore in another state.

Nights were the worst. The sounds, the crinkling of leaves and twigs, the strange nocturnal whispering all around him. He would lay awake in a furrow in the ground he had dug for himself, scooped out with his bare hands, a bed of leaves and twigs for a mattress, wondering if the same person was coming for him or if an animal was. Then again, in his mind, the person *was* an animal.

He remembered watching some guy on cable. An ex-SAS, piss-drinking, Everest-climbing, scorpion-eating British adventurer who would show you how to survive in the wilderness with nothing at all. As he watched the series, almost like osmosis, his brain slowly began to absorb some of the survival tips and strategies. He wasn't going to build an amazing tree-house shelter out of leaves and branches, or catch a fish with his bare hands, build a fire, gut, cook, and eat it. But what he had learned from the British guy meant he wasn't going to die of hunger, or from thirst, or exposure out here in the wilderness. He would live through this, find a way out of his predicament. He was determined to. Sure, he wanted to see his friends again, see his parents, not die in some muddy ditch only to have his remains picked clean by the animals and microbes, leaving just his bones for others to find. He would not become bone-dust to be carried away by the wind.

Climbing the ridge had been a grinding, painfully slow, one-step-at-a-time test of endurance and willpower, clawing with his bare hands, fingers and knees shredded, leaving bloody fingerprints and smudges on the rocks. Maybe the person was following him, stalking him, hunting him by the bloodied trail he was leaving behind.

He didn't know. Didn't really care.

One time he had slipped, tumbled end over end back down, his momentum finally coming to an abrupt stop, courtesy of a large boulder, almost as though it had been placed there deliberately thousands of years ago. And if that boulder wasn't there, or even if it was there, but maybe a foot farther to the left or to the right, then he would have tumbled right past it—and over a cliff edge, with the forest floor waiting for him a thousand feet below.

Another time during the climb, while he was resting, wrapping shreds he had torn from his shirt around his bleeding palms and raw knuckles, an unsettling feeling descended on him, as though someone was nearby, watching him. Turning and looking up the slope, over the rocks and gnarly bushes, he thought he saw someone standing above, peering down at him. A dark shape with the sunlight behind it. Quickly, he crouched lower between the rocks, held his breath, and closed his eyes. Then he stole another look up the slope, only to discover the person was gone, had vanished—if they were truly there in the first place.

He knew if he could get to the top of the ridge, then he could see where he was, try to pinpoint his location. *Get to the higher ground.* He remembered those words of advice from the British survivalist.

The last hundred feet of the climb was the easiest, not that any of the journey had been easy. His muscles ached, his knees, hands, forearms, and fingers were almost ruined. But they would heal with time.

Now perched on a rock, a few feet from the top, he could see just the sky above him, a wide canvas of blue. No more trees, nothing blocking his way to the summit.

He took a moment to steady himself, gather his reserves, build back up his resolve. He had done it, reached the top, just a few more feet now. He set off again, hands pushing down on his thighs, levering himself up, his breath ragged and labored.

Then he was there, at the top.

Slowly he turned and looked back at the panorama. The

valley spread out before him to the west. Beyond, the township sat nestled among the wilderness. It was too far to reach.

It was a mistake to approach the camp he had seen last night. He initially thought they were fellow hikers, could help him. Then there was the dog, a vicious, snarling thing that looked like it would tear him to shreds if he stepped any closer. After that, the man appeared. He was certain it was him, the same one, creeping toward him in the dark woods, searching him out. Could it be the same man? He couldn't see his face, but he was sure it was him, coming to finish him off like how he tried to previously. So he got out of there quick, ran as best he could, managed to escape for a second time.

Retreat was the only option. He wasn't ready to face him just yet. He was too weak, needed rest, medical attention. Then he would turn the tables on the man, go searching for him, become the hunter instead of the hunted.

To the south he spotted a smudge among the background of pale greens. It was closer than the town. Much closer.

Smoke.

He traced the smoke downward. It was rising from somewhere hidden below the canopy of trees. A campfire perhaps. A cabin maybe.

Judging from the distance, it was maybe five miles away, through thick forest and vegetation that would seem more like ten miles to walk. He noted the position of the sun, took a reading off the hands of his watch, memorizing the time of day. Then he worked out a rough bearing of the position of where the smoke was coming from so that when he descended back into the gloom of the forest, he could navigate toward it.

That's where he needed to go. Apart from the town, in the unreachable distance, there were no other man-made features to head toward. No obvious roads or trails or outposts. Just the thin, curling finger of smoke, beckoning to him.

Seeing the smoke lifted his spirits, bolstered his flagging determination.

He was going to die. We all were. But not today, tomorrow, nor the next day. He was going to get out of here, find his way back.

And when he did get out, climb out, even crawl out if he had to, he only had one thing he wanted to do. One purpose. And if he died the very next day, or even moments after he had completed that task, he would have fulfilled that sole reason to live that he so desperately clung on to now.

Then he would die a contented, happy man.

He was going to find the man again—and kill him.

That's all he wanted to do now.

Nothing else, including his own life, mattered.

# Chapter 34

After letting Ghost get a good smell of the shirt, Sam turned him loose, with them following behind, keeping their distance.

To Shaw, Ghost didn't follow any particular pattern. It seemed the dog was randomly running, then pivoting, stopping just to sniff and forage in forest debris before bounding off again.

While they watched on, Sam explained to Shaw the process. "There have been cases where dogs have found bodies in sixty feet of water."

"Underwater?" Shaw knew such dogs had a keen sense of smell on land, but he had no idea about them being able to detect bodies underwater.

"When a body is dumped in water, even if it's weighed down, gases will eventually escape and bubble to the surface," Sam explained. "While we, as humans, can't detect the gases because they could be parts in a million, dogs, because of their incredible sense of smell, can."

Shaw was in awe. Cadaver dogs could find human remains even from blood that was invisible to the human eye at a crime scene, where the perpetrator had tried their hardest to scrub every surface clean. But Shaw had no idea the extent of the sensitivity that canines had.

Sam went on to describe that when you see a dog at a water's edge, and it looks like the dog is biting and lapping at the air above the water, the animal is actually trying to almost "taste" the molecules of gases released from below the surface. Sam had often been called out with Ghost to conduct a water search for a missing diver or drowned person or a dumped body. Ghost would stand erect at the prow of the boat, chomping at the air above the water as the boat trolled the search area, hunting for the released gases of a decomposing body under the water.

"There was a case a few years back at a lake in Ontario where police divers spent twelve days searching the waters, looking for a young man who went missing after the canoe he was in capsized. When cadaver dogs were finally brought in, they took just fifteen minutes to find the surface location where his body was resting on the bottom of the lake below."

This was all remarkable to Shaw. He had worked with attack dogs in the past but not search-and-rescue dogs.

Up ahead he caught glimpses of Ghost as he worked through a spread of trees and low scrub. At times he could only see the dog's upright bushy tail wagging feverishly as he weaved back and forth through a plot of thick foliage. Then the dog would reappear in full, pause, rake at the ground before vanishing again. The dog wasn't just focused; it was like it was obsessed with finding the scent trail of Martin Fassen.

"How long will you let him search for?" Shaw asked Sam as they walked.

Sam didn't seem too concerned. "It depends on him. Usually, he will come back when he's exhausted the area. Then I'll take him someplace else and start all over again."

"Sounds like it's a waiting game."

Sam agreed. "You need infinite patience to do this. I usually use a GPS tracker, so I know what sections of search area we have covered so there's no overlap. But we have no clue if we are in the right spot at all. If this is a credible search area. It's all really guesswork at this stage."

"What about other dead things?" Shaw asked. "Like animal remains?"

"He can tell the difference between, say, the buried remains of a dead squirrel or raccoon and a dead hiker. They're trained to make those and many other distinctions."

Shaw nodded.

"Believe me," Sam continued, "Ghost, and all dogs like him can detect something as small as an old bone fragment buried many feet below the surface out here. Finding the scent trail of Martin Fassen shouldn't be too hard."

"That's if Fassen was here."

"Correct. That's if he was here." She stopped and turned to Shaw. "Like I said, we're going solely off your recollection of a woman's scream miles away while you were standing on a ledge looking out over the valley. The chances are extremely slim. The actual location could be as much as three, even five, miles. That's a lot of square miles, in my book."

Shaw watched as Ghost appeared again, ever enthusiastic and eager. Then he took off again, almost as determined as Shaw was in finding the missing couple.

"How will you know?" Shaw asked.

"That he's found something?"

Shaw nodded.

"He'll bark. Stay put in the location, and I'll go to him. Then we'll follow the trail." Sam continued walking. "Hey, look, I don't want you to get your hopes up about anything. We knew this was going to be a long shot."

"A *very* long shot," Shaw replied. He wasn't discouraged. "It's really good to just be out here, with you, and your dog, seeing what you do."

"What *we* do," Sam corrected him, a broad smile on her face. "We're a team, but he's definitely the star." It was refreshing to have a guy take a real interest in her work, her passion, her life's work.

175

Shaw watched then as the bright smile on Sam's face slowly waned a little as though a cloud had passed across her heart. Her mother. For a moment she was thinking about the search for her mother. Everyday spent here was a day not spent looking for Laura Rubino.

Then as quickly as it had appeared, the sadness vanished from Sam's face and she smiled again. "I'm glad I'm out here too. With you. I needed a change of scenery. I was getting into a rut. Same old, same old, as they say." She looked around. "I haven't been anywhere close to this place. I've never really explored this far into the valley before. It's a new experience for me too."

They continued walking, had only gone another hundred yards when, up ahead, the deep, throaty bellow of a dog's bark called out to them.

# Chapter 35

It was a piece of material, stained with blood, shredded and torn, part of a garment that had been ripped and discarded.

Sam knelt down and picked up the material with a twig, holding it up for Shaw to see.

"Blood."

Sam nodded. "But whose?" She looked around the ground, then turned to Ghost and made a noise with her mouth. The dog took off again, nose to the ground, searching the immediate vicinity, then gradually expanding in wider and wider circles.

Shaw searched as well, looking for any other traces that someone had been there.

Then Ghost barked again. Another piece of material, the same type as the first, this piece bigger though. It was stained with blood also. Sam cautiously examined the material, using a stick again to turn it over. The bloodstain was dark, had been dry for some time. Looked like it was torn from a sweatshirt, twill fibers.

Sam lifted the material and held it out to Ghost. The dog leaned in, his nose twitching, and he sniffed the scent, committing it to memory. He then looked up at Sam expectantly.

"Find," Sam said.

Shaw watched as the dog set off, nose to the ground, angling back and forth, trying to locate the scent trail. Then the dog's erratic movements straightened, and he began to follow an invisible trail away from them.

"He's got it," Sam said, pocketing the piece of bloodstained material. "Let's go."

Shaw dropped in behind Sam as they began to follow the dog through the woods, around trees, over logs, and fallen branches. After ten minutes the ground thinned, the debris less, and the outline of a trail appeared, barely visible through the undergrowth.

Ghost tracked forward, following the scent that was now cutting along the trail.

"She's been this way."

"She?"

Sam pulled out the shred of cloth. "Smell."

Shaw took the material and held it to his nose as he walked. "Perfume."

Sam nodded. "That's a bonus. Should be easier for Ghost to follow the distinct scent."

They kept moving, Ghost up ahead, trotting along the trail.

"Whoever it is, we need to follow this, find where Ghost takes us," Sam said over her shoulder as she walked. "It may be nothing or it may be something."

Shaw was happy to hang back, let Sam and Ghost lead. Judging from the jagged edges on the bloodied material, something violent had transpired, the garment ripped during a struggle or cut rough with a blade during an attack.

Ten minutes later, Ghost pulled up.

Sam stopped too. There was an object on the ground, pink. She squatted down, Shaw next to her. Lying on its side was a pink sneaker, a woman's size eight. On the rubber sole, in black marking pen were the initials, *KB*.

Ghost sniffed the sneaker, adding more scent to his memory before taking off again. Sam placed the sneaker in her backpack, then nodded to Shaw. "It's her, the German woman. Ghost is following her trail."

They didn't need any more confirmation. Karla Brigan,

possibly injured, bleeding, had come this way. As they moved through the woods, following the trail again, to Shaw it felt like they were heading back toward where they had come from yesterday, toward town and not deeper into the valley. They pressed on, not stopping, Ghost setting a relentless pace, the dog determined to find Karla.

The trail meandered through the woods. At times it vanished completely as thick foliage had grown over it. Then it would reappear again. Shaw sensed the trail was not used much, could see where grass and foliage had grown across the ground. It wasn't a common hiking trail. There were no markings or signs of overuse or deliberate grading of the terrain.

Ghost didn't pause or hesitate; he kept surging forward, following an invisible stream of molecules.

The descent down the ridge to the bottom had been easier than the climb.

He had made good time and had only stumbled once. At the bottom he made his way through the forest, checking his watch and the position of the sun every so often, making sure he was still on the correct course from the bearing he had taken from the top of the ridge.

A small running stream came into view, and he stumbled toward it, dropping to his knees to drink hungrily from the refreshing cool water. After drinking his fill and splashing his face and neck, he paused for a moment to check his arm. It still ached, and the swelling had increased, yet the pain was less. Maybe he was numb to it. Drink enough poison and you soon become immune to it until one day it finally kills you. That's what his grandfather had told him once. He had drunk like a fish and smoked like a chimney all his life, and died at the ripe old age of ninety-two. Resilience was part of the family genes, and he felt a surge of pride thinking back about his grandfather now. He would be proud of his grandson. But there was still more to do.

He touched his face. Despite the cool water, his skin felt hot and clammy, no doubt due to the infection. He had to go on, overcome whatever obstacles were thrown at him.

He stood and checked the position of the sun again through the canopy above. He was heading in the right direction, toward where he had seen the smoke rise from the trees. He struck off again through the trees, his pace quicker, feeling invigorated by the short pit stop by the stream. There was no clear trail, no path to guide him. However, luck was on his side. The terrain was flat, the vegetation not as thick as in other areas he had previously covered. This was a good sign.

An hour later he rested again, this time near a stagnant pool of water, a buzzing cloud of flies hovering above, and dragonflies skating across the murky green surface. His clothes were soaked with sweat, and his head throbbed. He could feel his body radiating heat into the air like a bad case of sunburn. During the last thirty minutes, the pain in his arm had been gradually increasing. Still manageable though. As he sat on a rock in the shade, with the tepid, cloying stink of the stagnant pool filling his nostrils, he thought longingly of the cool stream he had drunk from an hour ago.

Suppressing his craving thirst, he wearily got to his feet, checked his bearings one more time before setting off again. He sensed that he was close, close to the spot he had seen. Stay positive. That's what the British adventurer kept stressing. Everything that can go wrong will go wrong. All manner of things in the jungle will try to kill you, from the tiniest berry that looks so sweet, juicy, and appetizing to eat, to the largest, ugliest snakes on the planet that can kill you in seconds. You must stay positive. You must keep going. That's what he kept telling himself as he pushed on. Survival drove him.

That, and the almost unquenchable urge to find, then kill, the man who had done this to him.

# Chapter 36

She heard the lock turn, the hinges grind.

Bridget remained calm, motionless. She sat with her back against the wall, shoulders slouched, head tilted to one side, chin down, her chest rising and falling in slow, peaceful breaths.

She could sense him above her, pausing, looking down on her, doubt in his mind whether to come down the stairs or not.

Finally, she heard the clunk of the door being closed, the dull sound of feet as they descended each metal tread. Slower steps, though, almost cautionary. The sound of his reverberating feet not as loud as on previous occasions. Perhaps he was wearing soft-soled shoes this time, Bridget thought.

The air shifted at the bottom of the stairs. He had arrived, pausing again. Not coming forward.

Something was different. Not wrong. Everything was wrong. But now he seemed different. Bridget remained calm in her sleeping stupor. On cue, she began to snore. Nothing earth shattering. Just a low, nasally inhalation dragging the air across the roof of her mouth, followed by a soft but audible exhale.

Footsteps came toward her. Slow and measured. Almost a shuffle.

One, two, three she counted as she had done before.

Four. Five.

From the bottom, he always took, on average, eight steps to reach her. That way she knew the approximate distance to the stairs. There was little else to do to pass the time in this blacked-out hell she was in. Measure and imagine.

Eight. Nine. Ten? Eleven?

She sensed him standing in front of her now, over her, looking down at her like he always did.

Through the holes in the mask, Bridget caught the smell of something. She resisted the urge to move, her mind struggling to identify it. Subtle not overpowering. Not a fragrance. A living smell. Musty. Wet dog. Boiled cabbage and briny sweat. Grassy and greasy.

Apart from her breathing, Bridget lay perfectly still. Hands resting in her lap, the chain lying across one open palm.

She didn't move. Even when the strange smell intensified as he crouched down and reached out toward her.

She didn't move. Even when she could now smell his breath that reached out to her in raspy, tiny gusts. A sour, stale stink that had left a residual film on teeth and gums.

She didn't move. Even when she could feel the front of her shirt pry apart slightly from where she had deliberately undone an extra two buttons, revealing more of her cleavage, the firm curve of a young breast, enticing curious minds that had pure evil intentions.

Closer. Just a little closer. *You want to take a look, don't you? You can't resist.*

She pictured his head just inches in front of her. Saw where his neck would be in the darkness of her mind.

Closer. That's it.

Her palm closed silently around the chain and her fingers squeezed. The fingers of her other hand found and then slithered over another part of the chain, grasping it tightly as well.

*Now.*

Bridget exploded forward, moved with all the fury and rage she could muster, a blind person attacking their all-seeing jailer.

The chain came up in one horizontal line, her tight fists on each side, and she spun a hand over the head, like twirling a dance partner. Bridget drove her chest forward, her knees and feet scrabbling under her to get height, get leverage over him.

She heard him gasp in shock, not dying breath, then begin to fall backward, arms coming up to fend her off. Then a determined growl. Bridget kept powering forward, on her knees now, desperately trying to wrap the chain around his throat. One hand bound off a shoulder, a bony clavicle, thin necked. He fell backward, Bridget falling on top of him.

The side of her head went numb, as he punched out, a wild blow connecting near her eye socket. Her black universe exploded with a sprinkle of stars and comets. She ignored the pain, pressing forward. She was on top of him. With the chain in both hands, she began punching downward, raining blows on where she imagined his head was. Her right fist skidded off his cheek. Bridget's brain took a millisecond to adjust the next blow, conceptualizing the round dimensions of a small watermelon for a head. Her left fist, reinforced with the links of the chain, hit home, landing with a wet smack of blood and cartilage.

He tried to wriggle underneath her, get away, but her fury intensified and she shuffled farther up, her thighs pinning him in place, and began raining bombs, ground and pound.

He hit her again.

She hit him harder, faster.

Then he slowed, the fight draining out of him under the onslaught.

But Bridget didn't ease up, her knuckles raw, split, and bloody. The heat under the rubber mask intolerable, like she was drowning in a fishbowl of her own sweat.

Her hands found his throat, lifted the neck as she pivoted off him, looping the chain around, then crossing her fists, pulling tight. Arching her back, she dragged him backward, her feet hooking around each of his bony legs and pulling the chain with all her strength.

He thrashed about, a fish out of water, convulsing for air. Bridget held on, despite catching an elbow in the face. The blow was feeble.

Slippery, gurgling, choking sounds. The heels of his feet peddling and scraping the ground but not going anywhere.

She pulled even harder, gritting her teeth behind the tight rubber.

Then came popping sounds, cartilage crushing, the chain cutting deeper into his throat.

She could feel his body easing, the life draining, his heart slowing, the evil dying.

The thrashing fell to twitching.

The twitching eased into a few spasms.

The last spasm became a deathly stillness.

Bridget held on, not relinquishing her grip. She slowly counted to a hundred, then finally let go, kicked the body away from her.

She lay on her back until her breathing returned to normal, then rolled over and reached out with one hand searching. She felt a foot and she crawled over toward the body.

She started at the ankles, her two hands working in unison, fingers rummaging up each leg. He wore trousers. Past the knees, she located the front pockets, found a slight bulge in one. As her other hand scuttled across to join the other, her fingertips grazed a protrusion under the fabric, near the front zipper of the trousers.

She flinched with disgust.

Both hands were now working on the pocket, one tearing open the top, the other pushing inside. She pulled out a small bunch of keys. Three in total.

Painstakingly, Bridget knelt while reaching behind her head, trying each key in the padlock that held the mask in place.

The last key slid home. She twisted the key, and the padlock came undone and tumbled to the floor.

With the padlock off, she feverishly clawed at the buckle and undid the strap, then peeled, pulled, and finally wrenched the rubber mask off.

Shocking raw light hit her, and her world of darkness burned bright as the sun. Shielding her face, she waited until her eyes adjusted before looking down at the body in front of her.

Small. Wispy, gray hair. Bony arms and legs. Coarse, speckled skin. The body was lying with its back toward her. Bridget grabbed a bony shoulder and turned it over.

A face—eyes bulging from sunken sockets, blotchy and weathered, translucent with age, yellowed, brittle teeth with a purple tongue coiled to one side—stared back at her.

Bridget leaned closer, looked harder.

"Who the fuck are you?"

# Chapter 37

Using the same key as the padlocked mask, Bridget undid the manacles around her wrists and threw them at the wall in anger. She had been chained up like a dog, had some horrid rubber mask locked over her head. She didn't want to think what the man had intended to do to her.

But he was dead, and she was alive. That was all that mattered now—and getting out of this hellhole.

Try as she could, she couldn't recognize her captor. She searched the body one more time but couldn't find anything. No wallet. Nothing. Just the bunch of keys he had in his pocket. She looked at the body again. It seemed to have shrunken a little in the brief amount of time, shriveling almost in a time lapse, no longer a living, breathing person, just a husk, a vessel of evil. He was old, like really old. Bridget had expected someone else, younger maybe. That's the impression she got when he had visited those times, brought her food and water. Despite being unable to see and the fact that he had said nothing, instinctually, she thought he was younger, bigger, and more powerful. The man she had killed had put up a fight. No doubt about that. And yet Bridget was more than mildly surprised when she pulled off her mask and saw him for the first time.

Bridget rubbed her wrists, the skin almost red raw. Her face and scalp itched from the rubber mask. It lay on the ground, an ugly black thing, saggy, and deflated. She felt her face, puffy, tender, and swollen in places where the man had hit her.

The room wasn't a room at all, more like a sealed chamber

with high, smooth walls, overhead sodium vapor lights. No windows, just steel stairs leading up to a small gantry platform above and an open door.

The chamber was empty, except for an old portable generator and drums of diesel. Bridget didn't want to spend a single second in this place any longer. With the keys held tightly in one hand, she ran up the stairs and out the door. Through the door, Bridget found herself in a narrow corridor.

Wooden flooring. Faded yellow walls, decorative molding. She was inside a house. Someone's home. She paused, held her breath, and listened carefully, could hear the wind outside. The house creaked and settled around her. It was an old house.

She followed the corridor into a large kitchen, which looked like a museum exhibit, colors and styles from a bygone era. It reminded Bridget of her grandmother's house—after she had died. Pale-green laminate cabinets with tarnished chrome push-button latches. A heavy ceramic sink with big, old faucets. Plastic flooring in a repetitive octagonal orange, faded and blistered in places. A huge refrigerator sat humming in the corner.

The countertops were bare. The sink was empty. Looking out through the window above the sink, Bridget could see a red barn in the distance, the woods beyond.

Exiting the kitchen, she went back down the corridor, looking for the front door, any external door so she could get out of the place. She walked past closed doors, not bothering to see what was inside.

She reached the front door and heard the sound of a car pulling up outside, a low throaty groan of an engine. She backed up away from the door. Looking around wildly, she didn't know which way to turn. Someone was coming home. She needed to hide.

Where?

*Anywhere!* Her mind screamed.

Footsteps thumped up the front porch steps. Heavy, determined feet.

Bridget backed up some more, looking around desperately for a place to hide.

Too late.

The front door swung open. A person stood there, the light behind them, their shape just a dark, featureless outline. The person stopped when they saw Bridget. Their head tilted slightly.

*Fuck!* Bridget backed away some more; memories of the horrors in the chamber came flooding back to her. She wasn't going back, back to the rubber mask, and being chained up like an animal. This time she knew she would die down there in some utterly cruel and sadistic way.

The person stepped forward and into the house. Their arm moved, a hand grabbing at something on their hip, pulling out a boxy-shaped object, then shifting to a two-handed grip. They pointed it at her.

Bridget turned and ran.

She got three feet, then heard a pop from behind, followed by two sharp stings in the middle of her back before a crushing, muscle-cramping pain gripped her. She clenched her teeth, her eyes shut tight in sickening pain, before she fell heavily to the floor, her entire body rigid like a board.

# Chapter 38

He pulled her by the hair, her feet dragging behind, back along the corridor, past the kitchen, past the corner, back through the door, threw her down the stairs into the chamber, slammed the door shut, and followed her tumbling body down.

At the bottom of the stairs, he hauled her up by the throat— then stopped.

There was a body on the floor. Frail, shrunken, thin boned, with clothes that once fit, now loose and baggy. The curse of aging. The reverse of growing. Slowly you diminish, a shadow of your former self.

Dropping Bridget, Roy Beckman ran to where his father lay. Gently he cradled Floyd Beckman's head in his lap, stroked his face, and then began to weep. If only he had listened—his father—not to come down here alone, none of this would have happened. Tears rolled down Roy's face, onto his father's parched skin. His father wasn't as strong or as agile as he used to be. The passion, the will to kill was still there, burning hot and bright as it had when he was a young man. But now his body couldn't match that passion. So allowances were made. Techniques revised. Roy became more involved. Under his father's tuition, Roy learned how to select, stalk, hunt, and eventually take victims. Then, as his father deteriorated over the years, and his mobility became too restrictive to leave the house, to satisfy the urge, Roy became the courier, a delivery man of sorts. Like a parent bird bringing back food to the nest to feed their young, Roy ventured out to find the victims to bring back to nourish and satisfy his father's hunger.

Roy was introduced to his father's dark life at a young age, a life he hadn't known his father possessed. Roy had skipped school one day, decided to come home, only to find his father, who was sheriff at the time, in the kitchen standing over a young woman, gagged and hog-tied. The woman looked up at Roy Beckman, pleaded for her life with tear-filled eyes. Then Roy had done what any abnormal son would have done for their murderous father. He helped him carry the woman down to the bomb shelter that was built under the house by the original owner when the foundations went in. It became their killing chamber, and that day was a turning point for a young, impressionable Roy Beckman.

From that point onward, they were a team. Master and apprentice. Father and son spending quality time together. Floyd soon realized that the acorn didn't fall far from the tree. And just like his father, outwardly, there were no signs of the true evil depravity that lurked deep inside Roy. Far from it. First as a sheriff's deputy, then as the sheriff of Bright Water itself, Roy was a popular, likeable figure around town, just like his father had been. A hardworking pillar of the community who occupied the front pew of the church on a Sunday, sitting next to his father and mother. Outwardly respected, two generations in law enforcement. No one knew they were a father-and-son, murderous tag team who abused the trust that came with donning the uniform and wearing the badge that afforded them countless opportunities to easily stop and detain their unsuspecting victims.

They had agreed on a division of labor: Roy would watch and learn and dispose of the bodies. Floyd Beckman would find and usually kill the victims. On a few occasions, just to mix things up, and to give his son a taste, Floyd would allow Roy to "learn the ropes"—literally. With the victim bound and a strangulation rope around their throat, he would pass the ends of the rope to his son, to let him finish the task. Floyd stood watching, appraising Roy, giving him pointers on his technique, how to control the victims as they struggled, and the finer points of brink and release, the subtle art of slowly killing someone over a period of a few hours or an entire afternoon, if you wished.

Roy turned, looked at the fallen, twisted shape of Bridget. Then he spotted on the floor a length of wire with a wooden handle at each end. Another adaptation Roy had created for his father's fading strength. No longer did Floyd Beckman have the strength and vitality to wield a rope to strangle his prey. While tying a thick knot in the middle of Floyd's favorite piece of rope had made the job of strangulation easier for his father, his declining health and strength had left Roy with no alternative recently but to design a less strenuous but more efficient method of killing. The garrote was a simplistic design Roy had taken off the internet and was fashioned from hardware he had lying around the house. Like a toddler not willing to relinquish a well-chewed pacifier that was both a familiar symbol of comfort and security, Floyd was reluctant at first to give up the rope. Roy even had to confiscate any spare rope around the home, only to find that his father had somehow managed to find another length in the barn or in the discarded trash. However, after having no choice but to use the garrote on a bound female, German hitchhiker Roy had brought home, Floyd soon got a twinkle in his eye with the new toy he had been given.

It seemed to give him a new lease on life, only increasing his appetite for fresh victims. It was as though Floyd Beckman, conscious of the time he had left on this earth, had a bucket-list figure in mind that he wanted to hit before God pulled the plug on him and sent him to hell.

Bridget began to stir. Roy looked over. Somehow his father must have found the spare key to the chamber, decided to kill her alone without his son being present. In his younger years, his father would've had no problem with such a young and virile person. But now with his father nearly eighty years of age, and with the recent onset of Parkinson's disease, Roy had insisted, as a precaution, that no one would be killed without him being present.

Roy placed his father's body down, took a deep breath, filling his lungs with venom, and then moved toward Bridget. She was a mistake, would be missed by the townsfolk. He had never taken anyone so close to home before. Usually the victims were people passing through the county. Tourists. Travelers, people with no direct link to the town. But his father had been most insistent. Floyd had despised Carol McKenzie, Bridget's mother, for years. She was another one of the women in Bright Water from Floyd's youthful past, who had rejected his philandering advances. So Floyd decided to leave Carol McKenzie with the painful memory of her missing daughter as a gift during her retirement years.

Bridget mumbled something that Roy couldn't decipher. Her eyes were still shut, and her head lolled to one side, one cheek flat against the cement.

Roy smiled then drew his knee up high, his heavy-duty boot poised over the side of Bridget's face, aiming the thick, chunky heel at the soft side of her skull, ready to smash and stomp her head into a bloody, bone-fragmented paste.

# Chapter 39

*Thank God.*

From where Martin Fassen lay hidden on the edge of the woods, he could clearly see the SUV parked in the driveway with the county sheriff's department decal emblazoned on the side.

At the rear of the property, there was a large red barn.

Martin staggered out of the undergrowth, clutching his arm. The infection had grown worse, and searing pain tore at the festering flesh wound where the knife had slashed him. He shook his head to clear the fogginess as a cold sweat trickled into his eyes and across his upper lip. The SUV loomed closer. The house in the background seemed quiet, peaceful, salvation only a few feet away. He pressed on, ignoring the pain and the jitteriness he felt. The sheriff would know what to do, would help him. Call an ambulance, take him to the ER. As Martin staggered onward, he saw himself perched comfortably in a hospital bed, with clean white sheets and fat, soft pillows. Tubes running into his arm, feeding him drugs, softening the pain, giving him strength, accelerating his recovery so he could then search the town, go looking for the person who had done this to him and his girlfriend. Tears welled up in his eyes, mixing with tears of pain, as memories of his beautiful Karla came sweeping back to him. The future he once saw, *their* future together, now taken away by a cruel, murderous man. He pushed aside the last image he had seen of her. Her body, facedown in the dirt. Her clothing, bloodied and torn. He felt giddy as he walked, delirious with relief and with the retribution that would soon follow. He would make things right. Karla's death, such a waste that would not go unpunished.

Reaching the side of the house, Martin paused for a moment to regain his composure. His mind was swimming, the sky swirling. The air was cool, but his skin was hot and clammy. He tried to call out for help to anyone inside the house, but his throat was parched and ragged. All he could muster was a raspy whisper. Steps at the front led up to a wide porch that ran the length of the front of the homestead. Grabbing the railing with one hand, Martin hauled himself up, one step at a time. The pain in his arm was excruciating, like a blowtorch had been taken to it. But self-preservation was a powerful natural drug, able to dull the suffering he felt, driving him onward. Reaching the top step, he paused again, his breath ragged, his face, back, and chest covered in a sheen of perspiration. He felt woozy. The infection was raging inside him, his antibodies putting up an honorable fight.

He gazed at the closed front door, steadied himself, and then stumbled toward it. Only a few more feet, he told himself, and it would all be over. Help was just moments away. Reaching the door, Martin banged into it, unable to control his desperation. The door swung open, and he tumbled through, falling heavily on the floor, crying out in pain.

Down in the chamber, Roy Beckman glared up at the ceiling. Someone was upstairs. *Inside* the house. With his eyes fixed to the ceiling, he lowered his raised foot. Killing Bridget McKenzie could wait. Slowly he walked toward the stairs. He was certain he had locked the front door. Maybe he hadn't? After the initial shock then subsequent haste to incapacitate Bridget, he figured he must have closed but not actually locked the front door. On his duty belt, he wore a standard-issue Taser and a Glock 22, more than enough firepower to put down any intruder.

Gritting his teeth, Martin rolled onto his back, brought his eyes into focus, and stared up at the rose-pattern design of the light fixture above his head. He struggled to his feet. His injured arm hung by his side like a broken wing. He wiped his eyes, squeezed them shut, trying to shake the blurriness out, then opened them again. He was in a long hallway, old faded carpet running down the middle, faded walls. Martin edged forward, thinking surely there was someone home. He'd seen the SUV parked out front.

The unfamiliar slowly became the familiar.

They were coming from a new direction, a different angle, but everything around them now took on a recognizable feel. A particular pattern of trees. A cross trail. A distinct gnarly stump. Small clearings they passed. Ghost was out ahead, leading as he had done for the last two miles, no deviation in his speed or direction. Thankfully, the ground was flat, no real undulation, no rock barriers, drop offs, or heavy bush to wade through or circumnavigate. Shaw only had a light sweat, the air cooler and more refreshing under the canopy.

A smudge of red filtered through the trees ahead, and his heart quickened. They were approaching the barn on the Beckman property from the east, not the west as they had done before.

"You're kidding me," Sam muttered.

Shaw grabbed her arm. "Wait."

Sam called Ghost in. The dog broke his hunt, turned, and trotted back to her side. "The trail leads here. To Roy Beckman's property."

Shaw nodded. "Roy Beckman didn't just find the backpack belonging to Martin Fassen. He took it."

Slowly, it dawned on Sam. "So where is Martin Fassen? Why couldn't Ghost track his scent? We had his shirt."

"Because Martin Fassen didn't come this way. Karla Brigan, his girlfriend, did. They were separated. Tatters from her bloodied shirt. She left a trail through the forest leading to here."

"But why here of all places?" Sam whispered. "It was almost like she was following a direct trail through the woods. How did she know where she was going?"

Shaw thought for a moment and then said, "It wasn't her—leading the way."

Sam gave Shaw a perplexed look. "You said we've been following her trail through the forest. Her blood scent."

Shaw nodded. "We have. But someone had taken her. Was *carrying* her. Had brought her here, dead or unconscious, I don't know. Whoever it was, headed directly here, with Karla." Shaw nodded at the house past the barn. "And that person lives right there."

# Chapter 40

Quickly, Roy chained Bridget back up to the wall, rummaged through her pockets and found the set of keys she had taken from his father.

The time for grieving would come later. All that mattered now was finding out if someone was indeed inside the house. If someone was, then he would have to deal with them. He rarely had unannounced visitors. That was the appeal of the isolated location. If it was a parcel, then the delivery person usually would leave it on the front porch. No. The sound had definitely come from inside the house, near the front door.

He left his father where he lay and climbed back up the stairs, pausing at the top to listen for any sounds coming from the other side of the door. Nothing. He reached out and cautiously twisted the handle and slowly opened it, glancing into the hallway beyond. He couldn't hear or see anyone. He glanced over his shoulder at Bridget who was moaning now, rolling around on the floor, chains clinking. He would return later to deal with her. He was going to do something special with her while she was fully conscious. It was going to be a slow, painful, and very brutal death, just as it had been for the German woman. He still had enough plastic sheeting to cover the mess on the floor.

---

Martin found the kitchen, went straight to the sink, turned on the faucet full blast, bent down, and thrust his mouth under the stream of water, drinking greedily. When he was done, he wiped his mouth, the front of his shirt soaked with water. The kitchen was old, with a large refrigerator. He paused, listening. His throat was feeling better. But for some reason, some inner warning he felt, he'd refrained from calling out, seeing if anyone was home. He would search the house instead. His arm still ached. Maybe there was some ice in the freezer of the big old fridge. He was burning up; a fever raged inside him, the infection from the cut tearing through his bloodstream.

He glanced at the huge, old refrigerator. The appliance emitted a soft, innocent hum from the compressor at the rear.

Martin walked over and stood in front of it. Two doors. Two large chrome handles. Fridge section below, taking up two thirds of the capacity. Freezer above. He reached for the top handle, the freezer, and pulled it. The latch clicked and released. He felt resistance, and then heard a hiss, and a sticky, sucking noise as the seal of the door peeled reluctantly away from the main body. The door swung on large, well-oiled hinges. A blast of cold air and mist wafted out, hitting Martin in the face.

The cold mist began to dissipate. There were bags of frozen vegetables stacked neatly on the top shelf. A pint of Ben & Jerry's, Chocolate Peanut Butter Split. Tendrils of cold, icy mist continued to pour out as Martin stood holding the door open. Frozen dinners. Prepackaged meat. Icy food scraps in knotted plastic bags.

The mist cleared some more from the lower shelf, and...

Horror gripped Martin.

There on the bottom shelf sat the frozen head of Karla Brigan, eyes glazed open, mouth gaping wide, icy tongue twisted and protruding like a frosted blue serpent.

He stumbled back in fright, the freezer door still open, Karla's frigid stare following him, misty white hair-like tendrils flowing around her face, then reaching out toward him, a face that was contorted into a dead icy howl.

The sound of footsteps came down the hallway toward the kitchen. Martin spun his head around wildly, his mind caught between the gut-wrenching anguish of seeing Karla's face and the blind panic of what to do next.

Someone was coming. Big heavy footfalls.

His brain went into overload, couldn't process the raw stimuli fast enough. Frozen head? Footsteps? Sheriff? Friend? Killer?

Roy Beckman turned into the kitchen, saw Martin standing there, a shocked expression on his face, the freezer door open.

Martin's eyes cut to Roy, recognizing the face but not the uniform. The man who had killed Karla, the love of his life. His future wife. The man who had slashed out at him with a knife, slicing open his forearm, then chased him through the woods, ready to finish the job, was standing there, only a couple of feet away.

The circuit breaker in Martin's brain tripped. Cold reality and raw survival kicked in. He lunged to the side countertop, to a knife block. Eight inches of serrated steel came out in a bright blur in his hand.

It took Roy Beckman a few precious seconds to register who Martin was, put two and two together, and still not comprehend how the German backpacker came to be standing in his kitchen.

Fuck the Taser. Roy's right hand went to his holster, fumbling the draw, the heel of his hand catching on the back edge of the handgun.

Martin lunged, stepped in tight, slashed wide and long, opening up Roy Beckman's throat. Hot velvety blood sheeted out. Bright oxygenated crimson splashed across the white tiled walls, abstract patterns Jackson Pollock would have been proud of. One hand died gripping the beavertail of his gun, still snug in its holster. The other hand went instinctually to his throat, a pointless act to stem the flow. Blood pressure dropping. Heart pumping faster to compensate. Two natural but competing forces.

Martin didn't stop there, attacking Roy's chest in a frenzied stabbing motion, perforating him with deep plunges until Roy fell to his knees, then toppled over into a bloody pool. Martin stood over Roy, his own face crisscrossed red, the whites of his eyes behind a bloodied mask, his chest heaving from exertion.

Roy's body kicked once, quivered twice, then was still.

Without looking, Martin closed the open freezer door with the back of his hand, shutting off Karla's icy stare, the kitchen knife still clasped in his hand. Slowly, he surveyed the mess around him. The space resembled the aftermath of a red paint bomb exploding. Countertops pooled, walls dripped, the floor sticky and glistening. The fingers of his hand relaxed, and the knife clattered to the floor. He still had to process what had just happened. It was as close to a near-death and out-of-body experience he would ever have for the rest of his life. He had never killed anything before, let alone a person. Maybe a spider once. Oddly, he smiled at the memory, pictured Karla clad in nothing but a bathrobe, huddled in the corner of the tiny bathroom of her Munich apartment, pointing at an eight-legged thing on the wall, hysterically screaming for him to kill it. So he did. He would do anything for her. Red tears ran down his face. Now she was gone, and the last memory he would have of her was what was in the freezer. It would haunt him for the rest of his days. What kind of person does something like that? He glanced down at the body at his feet and saw the answer. He'd killed a sheriff. He was going to go to jail. Martin didn't know what the future held for him, let alone the next twenty-four hours. It was too much to comprehend. But one thing was certain. He was going to find the rest of her, of Karla. That was the right thing to do. Her parents could never know. He would insist on it. One person tormented by such a ghastly sight was enough. He was young, had more time to get over this. Karla's parents didn't. The death of their daughter was enough suffering for them. They didn't need to know the gory details.

Martin walked out of the kitchen, bloody footprints in his wake. In the hallway he cocked his head, could just make out the faint sound of a woman screaming.

# Chapter 41

The front door was wide open.

Sam glanced at Shaw. He held up a cautionary hand. Ghost growled behind them, then barked. Sam tried to hush the dog, but suddenly Ghost was going insane, barking, growling, panting hard, distressed and anxious all at once, his dark watery eyes transfixed at some point beyond the gaping doorway, deeper into the gloomy interior. Something was amiss inside the house, the dog smelling things that humans couldn't. Sensory overload.

Shaw eased through the doorway, saw the twisted hall runner. He edged forward until the archway opened up and he could see into the kitchen. Blood and gore everywhere. Roy Beckman lay facedown, a knife beside him. No need to check a pulse. From the quantity and locality of the majority of the blood pooled on the floor, he'd had his throat cut. Would have bled out in a matter of seconds.

Shaw glanced back at Sam and nodded. "Leave the dog." Shaw didn't want what appeared to be a crime scene, compromised. He remained outside the kitchen but continued looking in, noting everything that he could. The placement of the body. Blood spatter. The position of the knife. Even noting the time on the clock on the wall. It would all be important later. Statements would be taken. Observations scrutinized, tested, confirmed, or discredited. A trail of bloody footprints stepped away from Shaw, leading farther down the hallway. He felt Sam at his back, heard her gasp as she looked into the kitchen. "Get your cell phone out," he said, his voice low. "Touch nothing.

Step only where I step. Record everything."

Sam nodded. She panned her cell phone around the kitchen as best she could without actually stepping onto the kitchen floor, zooming in on the body of Roy Beckman and the bloodied knife.

Without saying another word, Shaw edged along the wall. He kept well away from the bloody footprints that seemed to fade with each step he took. Sam did the same, following in Shaw's steps, hugging the wall, skirting around the bloody trail as she continued recording. She glanced back at Ghost through the open front doorway. He sat on his haunches, his leash tied to a post. The dog whimpered. Sam gave him a reassuring nod, letting him know she was okay. Everything was okay even though everything was mayhem and carnage.

Ahead, one door was ajar, the doorknob coated in red. Shaw pointed at the red handprint on the wall, and Sam brought the viewfinder on her cell phone up on it. Voices came from the gap in the door, echoed and panicked. Shaw nudged the door open with his toe and stepped through, Sam bunching up behind him. They were standing on a small steel platform, at the top of a deep chamber, smooth walls, high-pressure sodium vapor lights hung from long cables, and steel stairs led down to the floor below. Shaw looked down, Sam next to him, tilting her cell phone around before settling the viewfinder on the scene below. Two faces looked up toward where Shaw and Sam stood above. Shaw recognized the man and the young woman. Reasons as to why they were here were unimportant. What was important was getting them out of there. He also saw the body a few feet away from where Bridget McKenzie was chained to the wall. Judging from the age and appearance, Shaw guessed it was Floyd Beckman. Father and son were dead, and dead for good reason.

"Follow me down," Shaw said to Sam. "Keep close. Don't stop filming. Miss nothing. Film the body as best you can, but don't touch it."

"I know what to do," Sam replied, her voice terse.

They descended the stairs, Shaw with his hands raised. He'd seen the knife in the kitchen that Martin Fassen had dropped, but he didn't know if the young man had another weapon. The last thing he wanted was the German to turn on him and Sam in his heightened, defensive state. Adrenaline would be coursing through him, his heartbeat would be elevated, and his sense of distrust of everyone would be overriding everything else.

"Martin," Shaw said, trying to sound as nonthreatening as possible. "It's okay. Everything is fine. You're both safe." Shaw turned toward Bridget, who was pulling at the chain. "Do you know where the keys are, Bridget?"

"He took them," she stammered. "Roy Beckman. The sheriff. He kidnapped me from the parking lot near my parents' store."

Shaw glanced at Sam, who had the sense to step toward Bridget and film her outpouring of exactly what had happened to her. For Shaw this was important, to record the details while they were still fresh in Bridget's mind. Later, every law enforcement agency, including local police, the sheriff's department from neighboring counties, and the FBI would descend on the property. Shaw wanted footage of everything before the place became a multijurisdictional anthill.

"He killed Karla," Martin mumbled. He shot a look at Sam who was now pointing her camera phone at him. "What are you doing?"

Shaw stepped forward. "Building a defense for you. There are two bodies here. One is—was—the sheriff of the town, this county. The other was the past sheriff. Law enforcement don't take too kindly when their own get killed."

"He killed Karla!" Martin repeated, more forcefully this time, justifying what he had done in his own mind. "Attacked me too. Tried to kill me."

Shaw could see the young man was in a daze, trance-like, but getting agitated. He was in shock. Shaw nodded at Martin's arm that hung useless by his side. The cut was rancid-looking, the wound area swollen, the edges of the skin flared red and angry. "We need to tend to that wound." Shaw needed to find a first-aid kit. But first he needed to get the keys from Roy Beckman's body without contaminating everything. Shaw turned to Sam. He didn't want to leave her down here alone with Martin. Before he could ask her, she volunteered.

"I'll go," Sam said.

"Film what you do with the body, where you step, what you touch. It will be important later. You will leave evidence on him. I just want to make sure we can explain that later to forensics."

Sam gave a grim smile. Moments later she was gone.

Shaw turned back to Bridget. "You okay?"

She nodded reluctantly. She was shivering, going into shock as well. "Martin killed Roy. He just told me."

"I know," Shaw replied.

"He killed Karla, put her—"

Shaw cut Martin off. "It was self-defense, wasn't it, Martin?" Shaw gave Martin an intense look, feeding the young man a script he needed to repeat back to him, and many more times in the future. "Correct?" Shaw had seen the handgun and Taser on Roy Beckman's duty belt. How Martin Fassen managed to kill the armed sheriff with a kitchen knife would be the subject of much debate later. While things looked bad, very bad, that particular aspect was in Martin's favor when it went to court.

And it would. Martin Fassen would be prosecuted. The body of Floyd Beckman would require some explaining too. That could wait for now.

Martin nodded. "Yes," he finally replied, more firmly now, his senses and awareness of what was happening was returning to him. He was picking up on Shaw's hints. "He attacked me. Had a gun. I was unarmed. There was a knife nearby. I grabbed it. Had no choice."

"Do you have any other weapons on you now?"

Martin shook his head.

Shaw was glad. Martin's attack was frenzied, and overly violent from what Shaw had witnessed in the kitchen above. There was more to this story. For the time being, Shaw pushed that and many other questions aside.

Sam returned with a bunch of keys and handed them to Shaw. She filmed him while he cycled through them before finding the right one, then freed Bridget from the chains. Shaw turned to Sam, looked at her sternly. "Make the call. Go back upstairs, out to the front porch, then wait for them. They know you. It's your town. Explain to them what they are going to find inside the house. Tell them that no one inside is armed. Tell them there are two dead perpetrators and two victims still alive that need immediate help. When they come, make sure they don't touch or contaminate anything. Guide them back down here if you have to. I've seen enough small-town police officers mess up crime scenes."

Sam looked into Shaw's eyes. "What about you?"

Shaw looked at Martin and Bridget. "We'll all be waiting right here." Shaw thought for a moment and then spoke again. "Then I want you to call a number. A guy called Dan Miller will answer. Don't tell him my name, just tell him that he needs to contact the nearest FBI field office to Bright Water and get a team here ASAP." Shaw gave Sam the number from memory, and she saved it in her cell phone. Shaw had never formally met Dan Miller before, but had been given his cell number by Carolyn Ryder, another contact of Shaw's inside the FBI he had had an intimate relationship with. However, Shaw didn't want to call Ryder on this. Past relationships are best left in the past.

He had the distinct feeling they were going to find a lot more on the Beckman property than just two dead bodies.

Shaw touched Sam on the arm. "Now go."

# Chapter 42

They came from everywhere, such was the alarm raised when two dead sheriffs, one past serving, one present, had been found on a property in the small town of Bright Water, sixty miles north of the state capital, Concord.

Few knew where the town was. Many had to look it up on a map, surprised when they finally located it nestled near New Hampshire's White Mountains in Grafton County.

First on scene was part-time officer Brad Hazard from the Woodstock Police Department. Officer Hazard was enjoying coffee and blueberry pancakes at Peg's Restaurant, just off Lost River Road, four miles south of Bright Water, when the call came through from police dispatch. What had first been described as an "incident," soon escalated into a full-blown invasion of the Beckman property after Officer Hazard arrived on the scene. Hazard, just twenty-two years old with a young wife and newborn at home, had the sense to remove his boots and slip on nitrile gloves before entering the house and surveying the scene in the Beckman kitchen.

Later, when forensic technicians queried the sour pool of vomit they found at the base of the refrigerator that contained traces of partially digested blueberries, someone advised them that a young, curious police officer had opened the freezer, and had taken a look inside.

A lieutenant and two officers from the same department arrived next, together with paramedics from the Linwood Ambulance Service and a contingent of sheriff's deputies from neighboring Carroll County. Two troopers from the New Hampshire State Police, who were cruising on the I-93 just north of Ashland in their sleek, black-and-gold Dodge Charger, overheard the police dispatcher, and decided to speed north and take a look for themselves.

Both Bridget McKenzie and Martin Fassen were transferred to the local ER, McKenzie later discharged while Fassen was still being treated for a serious arm infection.

An FBI agent from one of the ten smaller satellite offices that serviced the four-state area of Maine, Massachusetts, New Hampshire, and Rhode Island, arrived midafternoon. After a detailed assessment of the scene, and from talking to various law enforcement officers present, the FBI agent gave a live-stream update to Special Agent Dan Miller back in Virginia. Miller caught a flight to Concord and arrived before sundown.

Portable lights were set up, and crime scene investigators worked through the night on the Beckman property and surrounding woods for several days, gathering evidence. Dan Miller interviewed Sam Rubino and Shaw separately, and Sam provided Miller with the cell phone footage she had taken, explaining in immense detail what they had discovered.

An excavating contractor with a backhoe was brought in and stayed for seven days digging up various parts of the property. Unfortunately, the rest of Karla Brigan's body was never found.

An entourage of local and network TV vans descended on Bright Water, and soon the town resembled Fort Lauderdale during spring break as news reporters and cameramen jostled for the best positions around town to shoot live updates. Townsfolk went about their business as best they could. Some enjoyed the attention, gave interviews about how shocked they were when learning the awful truth about Roy and Floyd Beckman. Others shunned the out-of-towners, openly arguing with them in the streets, saying they were invading their privacy and harassing locals. Some die-hard supporters of the Beckmans refused to accept what had happened, deflecting blame on some out-of-state serial killer who was abducting backpackers and hitchhikers in Maine.

The big news networks out of Boston, and finally New York, picked up on their affiliate counterparts, and soon national network news choppers were buzzing over the Beckman property, taking footage. Air support was brought in from state police to warn them off, and a no-fly zone was declared above the property and surrounding woods.

Local businesses thrived, and the town's economy received a much-needed cash injection. Motels were soon booked out, including the Holiday Inn Express, and restaurants filled. Journalists, news reporters, camera crews, crime bloggers, even budding investigative YouTubers needed a place to stay, food to eat, and copious amounts of coffee to consume, all while clambering over each other for the next exclusive interview or golden nugget of information that would break the investigation wide open.

The Beckman house and barn were peeled apart like an onion, one layer at a time. Floorboards were ripped up, drywall cut open, furniture pulled apart, and crawl spaces explored.

A forensic anthropologist was brought in from Maryland. With the backhoe operator watching on, happy to be collecting his hourly charge to stand around, she spent the first hour pacing out the entire property on foot before drawing a detailed map on her tablet. The terrain, for the most part, was flat with a gentle slope toward the barn at the rear. The ground was mainly dry dirt, worn scrub with a scatter of small shrubs and stunted trees.

However, what initially caught the anthropologist's suspicious eye had nothing to do with what could be seen—the physical. It had to do with the invisible. Nitrogen is the essential mineral that turns lawns green and makes plants thrive. Areas of the ground, perhaps no bigger than a single car garage, were covered with a relatively green layer of grass and vigorously growing weeds and had been left untouched by the backhoe operator. So bright orange plastic pegs were driven into the soft earth, marking the particular areas, three in total. Layers of topsoil were slowly and meticulously scraped away by the backhoe under her watchful eye and a gathering audience of inquisitive law enforcement officials.

The first burial plot unearthed the partially decomposing remains of several dogs. Veterinarian tests would later reveal that some dogs had been strangled with rope, some with a thin wire, like a garrote, almost decapitating the animal. Most of the dogs had been microchipped.

The dogs, like their owners, were all local. After the owners were contacted, it was estimated that the more recent, less-decaying dog carcasses that were buried at the top few layers had disappeared over a span of six months to three years. The carcasses retrieved from the deeper layers were estimated to have been buried as many as ten years ago. Further scientific tests would later conclude that the sedimentary-like burial plot of dogs was a chronology of experimental endeavors undertaken by Roy and Floyd Beckman. Over a period of ten years or more, father and son went about perfecting and refining various strangulation techniques and testing various materials on local dogs before applying the same to their human victims.

The second and third burial plots unearthed the true extent of the Beckman legacy. The second plot contained the partial decomposing remains of several human bodies. Once again, they were layered in sedimentary fashion like an archaeological burial time line. Forensic bone and decomposition testing would conclude that the victims' bodies were as recent as a few months old, to remains dating back as much as five years.

The third plot contained much older, commingled skeletal remains. It was a jumbled jigsaw of bones and fragments that had to be painstakingly photographed, measured, recorded then catalogued in situ and delicately exhumed, accurately segregated, then reassembled into full skeletons in an undisclosed federal forensics laboratory in Virginia. The age of these remains were estimated to range from ten years to well over forty years old.

In the barn they discovered an extensive hidden collection of strangulation ropes, some with knots, others without, together with garrotes made from various materials ranging from braided fishing line to piano wire. Blood and skin cell samples taken from the ropes were later DNA matched to some, but not all, of the victims' remains from the two human burial plots. Other DNA matches were made by cross-referencing samples to the national missing person database.

In a morbid twist of good fortune, no less than fifty-six missing person cases would eventually be solved from a total volume of earth no bigger than two standard-sized backyard swimming pools.

# Chapter 43

"Take a look at this, boss," Luke Ramirez, a junior agent, said.

Ramirez was sitting in front of a laptop computer, scrolling through security footage given to them by local police, who had graciously allowed Dan Miller and his growing team—currently just three—to set up a temporary operations base in a spare office at the station. Miller had taken an interest in two men who had been killed in a fight in an alleyway behind a row of stores across from the gas station. It was little, seemingly unrelated oddities like this, especially in a small town like Bright Water, that always piqued Miller's interest when investigating a larger incident in the same geographical area. Miller likened crime, especially the most hideous and cruel, to a big spider's web that was more far-reaching than initially given credit for. During the critical early stages, as an investigation is unfolding and taking shape, no detail is unimportant. Everything is connected, linked together. Something viewed as unimportant and irrelevant that occurred on one strand of the web, could have reverberations for another part. Ted Bundy was driving down a street in his Beetle with the lights off when a patrol officer happened to notice. When the officer ordered Bundy to stop, he disobeyed, and the officer arrested him for what initially seemed like a misdemeanor. The rest is history.

So Miller had tasked Ramirez with compiling, then curating, a list of other crimes and misdemeanors that had happened in the local area before and after the incident at the Beckman property. Given that not much happened in Bright Water, the list was relatively small, the most significant incident being that two men were killed while another was seriously injured in an apparent altercation in an alleyway behind a strip of stores in town.

Ramirez pointed to the screen, having watched the footage several times, and quickly filled Miller in. "The young guy facing the camera is Joseph Lombardi, son of Tony Lombardi, a local business man. One of the richest in the state, so I've been told."

Miller listened while Ramirez explained that three of the men with Joey Lombardi, two of which were now in the morgue, were employees of Tony Lombardi's ski resort. The third employee, the one who had survived, along with Joey Lombardi, was in the hospital. Miller had subsequently discovered that Tony Lombardi owned most of the commercial properties and was slowly raising rents and kicking tenants out. There were also rumors that Lombardi's company planned to bulldoze most of the town and build a new shopping mall and hotels.

Miller made a mental note and singled out Tony Lombardi and his company for further scrutiny by the FBI's white-collar crime division.

"How is this related to the Beckmans?" Miller asked.

Ramirez flipped open his notebook. "Spoke to a few locals, definitely not friends of Roy Beckman, the sheriff. They said that Roy Beckman seemed at times to be working for Tony Lombardi. That they were very close, seen together a lot. Some said the sheriff gave his son, Joey, favorable treatment, and would turn a blind eye when some of Tony Lombardi's men were exerting undue pressure on local business owners."

Maybe there is a link, maybe not, Miller thought. "What about the perpetrator? Any ID on him yet?"

Ramirez shook his head. He had tried to enhance the video

footage, but the facial image of the one who had killed the two men was still unclear. "Whoever it was, I wouldn't like to mess with him. He cleaned all three of them up in seconds, especially this big guy, at the end, with just his bare hands."

Miller watched as Ramirez played the footage again. The perpetrator was outnumbered, that was certain, and Miller could see there were no visible weapons involved. Joey Lombardi was standing safely behind the three men, arms waving about, like he was giving them orders. The "big guy" that Ramirez was referring to was an understatement. He was massive. And yet despite it being three against one, and the perpetrator looking like nothing special, certainly smaller than the other three, he had brutally and effortlessly killed two of the men, and condemned the third man to a wheelchair for the rest of his life.

Miller watched the last thirty seconds of the video at half speed. Two men lay on the ground, motionless; the third was crawling along the ground like an injured bug. Joey Lombardi began to turn and run just after the massive guy had his neck broken, but was promptly caught, tied with what looked like his trouser belt, and thrown headfirst into a dumpster.

"The strange thing is," Ramirez said after the footage had ended, "that local police interviewed Joey Lombardi, and he's refusing to say anything about the incident. Said it was a private matter."

"So no one has come forward?" Miller asked. "Volunteered any information?"

"No one."

This was certainly interesting for Miller. Obviously, there was more to it. He made a note to definitely get the bureau's other divisions to take a look at the Lombardi family. It was strange how one investigation often threw up clues as to other illegal activities that were going on around it. Maybe it would lead to something.

Miller patted Ramirez's shoulder. "Good work." Miller pointed to the grainy image on the computer screen of the man slowly walking toward the exit of the alley. "But I want to know who this guy is." Miller didn't know who he was, but his gut was telling him he had seen him or run into him before.

They agreed not to meet in town.

The place was overrun by law enforcement officers. Roadblocks had been set up with two police officers stationed along the only road that led to the Beckman property.

Sam had noticed a few news helicopters flying over the surrounding woods as well. So they met at her cabin, sat on the back porch, and watched the sun slowly descend among the trees.

"They've found bodies," Sam said. "A lot of them."

"So I've heard."

"And you were right about Floyd Beckman," Sam said. "It seems that he wasn't recently living in the house. It was just Roy who was."

"So where was Floyd living all this time?"

Sam was sickened by the revelation that Dan Miller had shared with her. "In a care home. Ten miles away. It looks like Roy would visit his father and take him out, back to the family home on weekends when he had a victim ready and waiting in that dungeon of theirs."

Shaw said nothing for a moment, his mind picturing the insidious nature of the father and son relationship. Floyd Beckman's "reward" or "treat" was not to leave the care home for a nice meal or day outing. It was so that he could strangle and murder more people. While most people Floyd's age were spending what precious time they had left with their grandchildren or doing puzzles, Floyd was still wrapping rope around people's necks and killing them—with his son's help, of course. Roy was continuing to feed his father's obsession, like how someone would feed their pet snake the mice they had diligently caught for it.

Sam took a deep breath as she watched Ghost perched on a rock, lapping water from the stream. "I can't do this anymore." Her words sounded small, distant. She turned to Shaw. "I can't. I'm sick of finding dead people. Now this, with Roy and his father. I'm surrounded by death. I close my eyes at night and see bodies in the ground, covered in mud and leaves."

Shaw listened patiently as Sam began to let go of all the anguish that was built up inside her for all these years. "I'm sick of looking at the dead, finding them. I know it's important, that it gives closure to the families. But ..." Her voice trailed off.

Shaw touched her leg. "You do good work. You do things that most people can't even begin to think about. You're a strong woman."

"I thought I was—strong." Self-doubt now crept into her voice.

"A lot of good comes from what you do."

"But not enough good. The wins are few and far between. Most of the time it ends in heartbreak."

"What about that young girl, Millie Walker? You saved her life. Her father was going to kill her."

Sam gave a forced smile. Cases like Millie Walker were, at times, lately, the only thing that was keeping her going. But there weren't enough happy endings for her. And now it was looking

218

like, perhaps, Floyd Beckman had a hand in her mother's disappearance. Dan Miller had said to Sam that they hadn't identified all the bodies discovered on the Beckman property; there were still a few unsolved, especially the older ones. She hadn't told Dan Miller either about her missing mother, the dread she felt with every passing day of a phone call, telling her that they had found her mother, or what was left of her, mixed in with the remains of others. She gathered that he probably knew about her missing mother, anyway, from researching into her own background as well as talking to the locals.

In the last few days, Sam had become withdrawn, depressed that there was a distinct possibility her mother was dead, was one of the Beckman victims. It seemed like the only logical outcome now.

"Bridget McKenzie seems to be doing well," she said, changing the subject. "Just a few minor injuries." She looked at Shaw again, and her mood brightened. The simple action of just looking at him somehow always made her feel better, less stressed, happier. "She asked about you." Sam allowed herself a smile and put on a young girl's voice. "Asked about 'the intense man with the handsome face' who saved her."

Shaw gave a slight smile. "I saved no one. You and Ghost led us there. She saved herself, killed Floyd Beckman, and freed herself. Martin also played a part."

Sam slinked her arm through Shaw's arm possessively, and gently rested her head on his shoulder. "You are my 'intense man with the handsome face,' and I'm not sharing you with anyone."

They said nothing for a few moments, content with each other's company and watching the last rays of sunlight sluice through the trees.

"It's ironic, don't you think?" Sam spoke, her eyes closed.

"What is?"

"How Bridget McKenzie and Martin Fassen, who almost became victims themselves, ended up killing both Floyd and Roy Beckman."

Shaw gave a shrug. "It's funny how the world works at times. The Beckmans both got what they deserved, justice at the hands of their victims, or potential victims. That is the sweetest justice of all."

"And here I was thinking there was no justice in the world."

"How so?"

Sam sat upright. "If they hadn't been killed, that is, if they had been caught, they would have spent the rest of their lives in jail, getting three square meals a day with all the comforts paid for by the taxpayer." Sam looked Shaw in the eye. "I'm glad they're both dead."

"What about Martin?" Shaw asked. Shaw had kept a low profile during the investigation. He didn't want the attention. Shaw had been interviewed by Dan Miller, who mentioned nothing about Shaw's background, despite Shaw knowing that Miller would have done a thorough background check on everyone involved.

"He's been released. But he can't leave the state until the investigation is concluded."

"That could take months."

Sam nodded. "Apparently Karla Brigan's parents are flying in from Germany. So are Martin's. The story is in all the German newspapers and news websites."

"He'll be fine. You gathered enough evidence on your cell phone."

"So what happens now?" Sam asked.

"With what?"

She gave a skeptical look before pointing her finger back and forth between them.

"What do you want to happen?" Shaw asked.

The late afternoon sun was low, bathing the treetops in a honey glow, throwing the first of the long shadows toward where they sat, announcing the arrival of dusk and the impending night.

Sam edged closer, wanting to feel his warmth on her. She tugged at his arm. "I want you to come inside."

# Chapter 44

Ghost didn't bark.

There was no need to. The woman wasn't a stranger to him. He knew her. He knew her smell, her particular scent, the touch of her hand across his fur. The particular way she stroked his head, the same hands that fed him treats sometimes when he ventured deep into the woods foraging and searching. At times she would feed him too much, so that when he returned home, he would be disinterested in dinner. He knew the sound of her voice, the way she spoke to him, traces of tone and pitch that he recognized from someone else's voice. He could sense things about the woman, too, in that unexplainable way dogs could sense, which science couldn't even explain. She also shared the same DNA as someone he knew very well.

Three weeks had passed since the news first broke. That was enough time, the woman thought. She had read the newspapers, watched the daily headlines, kept a keen interest as more was revealed about the ongoing investigation, gauging the barometer of public sentiment as to what had transpired on that property in the small town of Bright Water, for so many years. And as more horrific details came to light, even she was shocked as to the extent of the murderous acts of evil from the father and son duo that lived in plain sight in the small mountain community.

She needed to know for certain if it was true, that they were both dead, that the years of hiding in constant fear had finally come to an end. It wasn't her own safety that she was concerned about during that time. It was fearing for another—her daughter.

It had always been about Samantha, doing whatever she could to protect her, even if it meant living a life in exile, far but not too far to observe from a distance.

So she had moved away, fled to another county, assumed another identity. But she had still followed her daughter's growth from a young child into the beautiful adult woman she was today. As a mother, she was proud of what Sam had done, the career she had chosen. And for all those years, her heart ached at the thought that the true person her daughter wanted so desperately to find, didn't want to be found, had deliberately remained hidden—until now.

The family legacy of horror was no more, and that gave the woman solace to step out from the darkness and into the light, to reveal herself, despite thinking a day like this would never come. While in exile, she often wondered if the day ever did come, how she would breach the divide that had taken thirteen years to build and widen.

But that day had arrived; the wait was over, and she was as ready as she could ever be. In her own mind, the simplest way was often the best. So she had waited until the man had left, made sure he wasn't going to return any time soon, because she needed time, plenty of time, to explain fully why she did what she had done.

She felt a wave of relief as she walked out of the darkened sanctuary of the woods and into the bright morning sun, finally throwing off the cloak of concealment she had worn all these years. It was good: to be herself, to walk unhindered, to hold her head high without fear or apprehension.

With decisive strides, she made her way down to the stream, traversing her way across, stepping on all-too-familiar stones, knowing which ones were firm and which ones would tilt under the slightest pressure of her toes.

Reaching the other side, she made her way up the slope toward the cabin, her eyes fixed on the rear door, watching for any signs of movement, apart from the spiral of wood smoke coming from the tin flue pipe in the roof. As she approached, her heart thumped a little harder, her breath drew a little shallower, her throat squeezed a little tighter, and her uncertainty spread a little wider in her mind. How would she react, the girl who had grown into a young woman? Would she forgive her, or would she disown her, like how she had done to her all those years ago?

Time would tell, time that was slowly running out with each step she took toward the door, counting backward in seconds now not years stretching forward as it had done.

Reaching the back door, she paused, the anticipation almost unbearable. Steadying her nerves, the woman reached out, then knocked.

Sam was standing at the map on the wall when she heard the knock on the door.

Ghost, from where he sat on the rug, raised his head and sniffed the air, then thumped. Sam watched him as he rose and padded over to the back door, dipping his head, then sniffing along the gap at the bottom. Sam frowned. Ben had left nearly half an hour ago after staying the night. They had agreed to spend the new day apart, alone, maybe catch up tomorrow.

Sam walked over to the back door, reached out, then paused, her hand just inches from the lock. No, she had a better idea.

Sam opened the front door and slowly made her way around the side of the cabin with Ghost ambling by her side. Sam rounded the back corner of the cabin and saw a woman standing there. Sam stopped, stood dead still. Ghost continued on, tail wagging, went to the woman, nudged her hand affectionately with his snout, licking her fingers with his tongue.

*Could it be?* Sam's heart soared so high she couldn't breathe.

No. It wasn't her mother. The woman looked nothing like her. Her hair color was different, for starters. Sam's hair was a lustrous red, like her mother's. Bright as fiery copper fresh from the furnace. This woman's hair was raven black, short, slightly unkempt, fashioned in a more dignified style, best suited for a woman of her age.

From its initial lofty height, Sam's heart quickly crashed and burned in a fiery heap in the pit of her stomach.

The woman finally turned toward her. Their eyes met. The same shade of emerald green regarded one other.

For the second time, Sam's breath vanished, was whipped away out of her chest. Sam didn't move, her feet remained rooted to the ground, her limbs had lost all function. She felt an uneasiness begin to build in her gut, a kind of fear of the unknown, of what had once been that could never be the same ever again. A fear of lost time and of uncertainty and how to replace it.

Laura Rubino slid her hand into her pocket, pulled it back out, and held her palm up. Ghost scooped up the dog treat, then sprang up onto his hind legs and rested both front paws on Laura's chest as he stretched to almost her own height. She kissed the top of the dog's head, the long-standing affection obvious between the two. "You kept her safe all these years when I couldn't," Laura said, tears in her eyes as she ruffled the sides of Ghost's head with both her hands while Ghost lapped her face with his big tongue.

Sam's heart tightened in her chest as a flood of mixed

emotions hit her all at once. She teetered slightly; she could barely stay on her feet as she recognized her mother's young face amid the added wrinkles, lines, and maturing features that thirteen years of absence had denied Sam the opportunity to watch unnoticed. Shock, confusion, disbelief, then anger, resentment, followed by love and devotion all became caught up in a tumbling menagerie inside Sam's heart and soul.

Ghost stepped down, and Laura held out her hand toward her daughter. "Samantha."

Sam went to her knees and wept.

The search was over. Mother and daughter were reunited.

# Chapter 45

They sat together on the rear deck and did nothing but talk.

The stream glistened in the distance and spoke in soft murmurs. The wind moved through the trees, and the gentle curvature of the sun marked the passage of time as it slowly arced across the sky. It was as if it were just the two of them on the entire planet as it gradually rotated. Morning soon transitioned into afternoon, and with it came a crisp breeze that gathered up the leaves and threw them along.

Coffee was replenished, shawls were brought out and draped over shoulders heavy with the burden of an uncertain future. Initial tears of joy gave way to the somber reality that things could never return to how they were. The life Sam once had with her mother was forever gone, condemned to past memories, replaced with something new, exciting, but also daunting at the same time. The woman who now sat beside her, while still retaining traces of the former version of her mother, was a new person, someone she had known but didn't really now know—if that made sense. Laura Rubino had been absent for more than half of Sam's life. And with that, came a whole set of complications.

"You're still my daughter," Laura said. "However, we cannot go back, pick up where we left off. What once was, is now gone."

Laura had to run thirteen years ago. She had no choice as she had explained to Sam. "Floyd Beckman was incredibly jealous. He constantly pestered me. Said that he was in love with me. Said we could run away, make a new start. He wanted me to leave you and Clint. When I said no, I saw another side to him. A side that I'd never seen before, a side that he'd kept hidden from the entire town. He became enraged, insane with jealousy. That's when he threatened me." Laura had explained that one night, the day before she disappeared, Floyd Beckman had paid her a visit, told her that if he couldn't have her, then no one could. "He said the town wasn't big enough for the both of us. So I had to leave, the next day. Tell no one, just go, vanish."

"And the threat?" Sam asked. "To kill you if you didn't leave?"

Tears began to fill Laura's eyes, not tears of joy on this occasion. "I wished it was that. But it was something much worse."

Slowly it dawned on Sam what that threat was, what had caused her mother to just up and leave the town with not so much as a word. Anger began to simmer in Sam. Anger and a little envy. She was envious that it wasn't her instead of Bridget McKenzie who had strangled Floyd Beckman. Envious that it wasn't her instead of Martin Fassen who had slit Roy Beckman's throat.

"He said that if I ever returned, if he ever saw my face around here, then he would kill you, hide your body somewhere so it would never be found."

Sam thought about this for a moment. Surely her mother could have done something. "Why not go to the police?" Sam asked. "Tell them what he had said, how he had threatened you and threatened to kill me, a twelve-year-old child."

Laura looked at her daughter, savoring being up close to her, being able to touch, hug, and finally kiss her instead of just watching in silence from a distance. Something that she had done for thirteen long, cold, lonely years. "He had it all figured out. Told me that night that if I did tell anyone, even the police, it would be his word against mine. He was the police; he was the sheriff—he was everyone back then. He was obsessed. When I turned him down one final time, he became truly evil and vindictive."

Her mother's reasons made sense to Sam. The world hadn't really changed that much in thirteen years when it came to making accusations against law enforcement. Townsfolk and other law enforcement officials certainly would not believe that such a fine, upstanding citizen as a town sheriff would make such horrific and manipulative threats. Unlike other law enforcement officials such as the local police, county sheriffs were a law unto themselves. No government supervision. Not answerable to a mayor or a city council. They were elected by the people for the people. Sam remembered vividly once when Roy Beckman—a deputy at the time—was running for election as the next county sheriff. There was a gathering outside the courthouse in town, Floyd standing next to Roy on a small stage that had been erected, arm around his son's shoulders, telling the smiling audience that to continue to keep the town safe and secure in the future as it had been in the past, they should vote for Roy as the next sheriff. It was a natural progression. Floyd had told the gathering to hand the "baton" of law and order from father to son. He was retiring to fly fish and spend more time hunting in the woods. The only continuation that Floyd Beckman had in mind was hunting and killing humans. And it now seemed to Sam that Roy had followed in his father's footsteps. It was an evil, horrid legacy.

Laura took hold of Sam's hand, brought it over to her own lap. "Please, look at it from my perspective. I didn't abandon you, Samantha. You must believe me. I had no choice, and I didn't want to risk him carrying out his threat. He was popular around town; everyone liked him. It would have been my word against his. The entire town would have been on his side. I'd be fighting against everyone."

"Did you know I was engaged to his son, Roy?"

Laura gave a dejected nod. "I found out."

Sam frowned. "How? How did you find out?"

Laura smiled. "I came back. I took the risk after ten years had passed. I thought it was time enough just to slip into town, under the radar."

"You came back?" Sam was confused. Why hadn't her mother contacted her? "Why didn't you come to me? Why didn't you tell me?" Sam demanded.

Laura shook her head. "It wasn't like that. I couldn't contact you. It was too risky. If I was recognized, you'd be dead. I also didn't know how you would react. That and ..." Laura's voice trailed off.

"That and the fact that you didn't trust me?"

Laura Rubino's shoulders slumped. It was the truth. The only person she could trust with her secret—was herself. She looked like a defeated woman. She wiped her nose, paused, and then gathered herself together again. This time when she spoke, her voice was broken. "I didn't trust that you would tell no one. That you would keep it to yourself. I was fearful that somehow, it would get back to Roy or Floyd that you had seen me, or that I was in contact with you." Laura's mouth began to tremble. "You have no idea what it's like to watch my daughter, my only child from afar. It was like I was standing on the outside of a cage, watching something so precious, so rare, and so endangered.

Tears filled her eyes again as she stared deep into Sam's own eyes. "Never to reach out and touch you. Never to feel the warmth of your skin on mine. Never to feel your heartbeat against mine. It was torturous. Yet I kept my distance, hid, and watched you in secret."

Now hot tears of sadness and frustration began to roll down Sam's cheeks. She had no idea that for all these years, her mother was watching her. As though from behind an invisible glass wall. Never to talk, to reach out, to touch. It was an altered reality, of insufferable pain and never-ending anguish.

"When Floyd Beckman finally retired and became housebound, I was more courageous. I would only cross the county line and come into town maybe once every few months. It wasn't like I moved back, Samantha, trust me."

"What about Roy Beckman? Did he know?"

"He was just a child like you when I left town. But I guessed that the threat was handed down from father to son, a vendetta being passed to the next generation. Everyone thought I'd run off with another man, so if I suddenly appeared again, news would make it back to Floyd."

Sam took a deep breath. It was so much to process for one day. "How did you do it?"

"Like how did I go unnoticed?"

Sam nodded. Her mother's raven-black hair was a clue, yet Sam wanted hear the full story, everything.

Laura touched a loose strand of her hair, trying hard to remember what it used to be like when she was a redhead. "I altered my appearance, covered my face when I could." Laura gave a forced smile. "Winter was always the best season to sneak in."

The remark made Sam smile. This was incredible.

"I was a stranger in the place, pretended to be a visitor, a face that blended in and could easily be forgotten. I gleaned what new information I could from people I didn't know. Being such a small town, it's amazing what people will divulge to you when they know you're just passing through. Local gossip and rumor. Who the new sheriff is. What happened to the old sheriff. Who's the local young woman who was in the newspapers recently about finding the bodies of two abducted children? What's she like? Have you seen her? Where does she live now?"

Sam stiffened. "So you were spying on me all this time?" She felt slightly shocked. Slightly betrayed. She pulled her hand away from her mother's lap.

"I didn't spy on you, Samantha. You must believe me. I wanted—needed to see you, without you seeing me." Laura was pleading now, fearing that the mother-daughter reunion was taking a resentful turn, something she had anticipated but desperately wanted to avoid.

# Chapter 46

Darkness came, bringing with it a cold chill, so they moved inside and sat next to the fire.

Sam had so many more questions that she wanted to ask, almost fearful that her mother would up and leave, vanish again. "What did you do for the last thirteen years?"

"I hid, Samantha, lived another life. But I kept watch on you." Laura Rubino gave a painful look, remembering all the years of waiting, hoping, unable to come back to her family. "It was torture." Tears filled her eyes as she regarded Sam. "The worst years of my life. I went to some pretty dark places, wanted to die one time." She rubbed the tears away and cursed herself for breaking down like this. "Like I said, it was only in the last three or so years that I took more of a risk. I would use the woods on the other side of the stream. I felt safer there, hidden. I only went into town a few times, found out what I needed, and left it at that. Change moves very slowly around here, as it had done before." Laura looked down at Ghost, who sat on the floor, equal distance between mother and daughter, his loyalty shared between them.

"Ghost saw you," Sam said. "You've been feeding him." Sam remembered when Ghost had returned from the woods and didn't want to eat his food.

Laura smiled. "He took an instant liking to me. He must have sensed that I was not a threat. Maybe he knew we shared the same blood, family. He was the physical link between you and me, something we both had touched even though I couldn't reach out and touch you."

Sam felt tears well up again in her eyes. No frustration this time, just daughterly love for her mother, a maternal bond that continued long after the cord was cut. "What about Dad? Did you see him as well?"

Laura shook her head. "No, I didn't. I knew it would have been hard on him too. I heard the rumors around town." Laura leaned forward. "I know this all sounds crazy. But I wasn't running from you both. I didn't walk out on him for another man. I had to leave, remain hidden for everyone's sake."

Sam said nothing for a few minutes, just watched the flames dance and glow in the fire. She knew deep down inside that nothing would ever be normal again. They would have to leave town, all three of them, move as far away from this place as possible. It was either start anew or be constantly in the limelight. Then again she had her own home now, her cabin that she loved so much, nestled in the woods next to the stream. She loved it there. Her place of isolation and solitude. Whether or not she could stay there in Bright Water in the aftermath was another thing, however. The future was just too uncertain that Sam didn't want to think about it. There would be changes though. She could find another place, another cabin. It wouldn't be the same though. One thing was certain; there was no going back to how things were. She was a grown woman. "You need to see him." Sam spoke again. "He took your leaving very bad. Began drinking heavily soon afterward and never really stopped."

"I know. I will go by and see him. I just wanted to see you first. In time, I will tell him. I will tell everyone, including the newspapers. I need to tell my side of the story so that everyone knows the truth. How evil Floyd Beckman and his son were."

"Dad will be pleased," Sam said. Maybe he would give up the booze. Get himself and his life back on track. A pressing question came to mind for Sam. "Is there anyone else?"

"Like another man, you mean?"

Sam nodded. "Thirteen years is a long time. Did you settle down with someone? Are there—you know, others?"

Laura's expression softened. "You are my only family, Samantha. There is no one else."

Sam felt relieved. It was just a crazy thought, if she had any half brother or sister, but she needed to know.

"And other men?" Sam noticed her mother hadn't answered the first part of the question.

Laura gave a sigh. "I've not remarried, if that's what you're asking." Then she looked away into the fire when she spoke again. "But like you said, thirteen years is a long time. I have a new life, moved to a new town, new job, new identity."

"A new life? What about Dad?"

Laura met her gaze again. "I met someone. Only recently. In the last few years. But I've told them nothing, about you, Clint, this town, and what happened." Laura reached out and touched Sam's arm. "Look, I don't have all the answers as to how this is going to work. We're going to have to play it one day at a time. This is going to take time. Others are involved now."

Sam pulled away, and Laura felt her heart tear. "Know this, Samantha. I never disowned you or your father. You will always be my daughter, and I'll always be your mother." Sam noticed how her mother kept saying, "your father" instead of "my husband." Laura Rubino, in part, had moved on.

"We'll get him all the help he needs. I promise. He is a good man and has suffered enough over the years. He deserves better."

Sam stared at the fire again as though all the answers were buried among the flames and glowing embers. It seemed like that for every answer her mother had given her, five more questions sprouted up, all equally as important and complicated to answer. Sam had waited this long; she could wait longer to figure this all out. It wasn't as simple as she had expected. She had prepared each day during the last thirteen years for her mother not to be there with her. She had prepared each time when she ventured out to search for her, planned each step, where she would look, tick off another wasted day, another wasted search looking for her. Even had planned for the worst case scenario—finding her mother's remains, just her bones or someone knocking on her door one day telling her that her mother's body had been found. But she had never planned for her mother turning up again alive, because she was so convinced she hadn't run off. Sam, all along, had expected the worst. Ironically, she had never planned for the best outcome. No one did. She had seen it enough times when she had been called in to find a missing person. Do your best, but expect the worst. Finding anything else was a bonus she kept telling herself.

"Life's not perfect," Laura said. "But we'll figure it out. All of us together."

Despite the detailed explanation Laura had given her, Sam was still left with a lingering anger and the feeling of abandonment. Why couldn't her mother have taken her with her? Why couldn't they have escaped the town as a family, all three of them? Maybe it was that Floyd Beckman wanted to destroy what her mother had: a happy marriage and devoted daughter. He wanted Laura to leave them behind to suffer in the anguish of not knowing, and for all of them to be tainted by malicious gossip and innuendo in the aftermath.

It was far worse than if Floyd Beckman had just told Laura to up and leave with her family, to move to another state far away from him. No. Floyd Beckman wanted to enjoy watching the years of torment Sam and her father would go through under the design of his evil, vindictive plan.

Sam looked again at her mother, saw the eyes she had remembered so well when she was a child. Kind, understanding, full of love and devotion for her—that couldn't be taken away. Sam moved closer and fell into her mother's arms, her own body fitting perfectly into her mother's embrace. It didn't feel foreign or awkward.

It just felt right, in this moment.

Forgiveness would come later.

# Chapter 47

"It will take time, I know," Shaw said.

They were sitting on the back porch of Shaw's cabin; the sun had just come up. Sam hadn't slept at all. She and Laura had stayed up the entire night talking, reminiscing, crying, and even laughing at times. Making up for the lost years, and there were plenty of them to make up for.

She had told Shaw everything even the confusion and uncertainty she now felt.

"But you have time, Sam. The three of you need to spend time together and sort this out."

"It's going to be a circus when news of this breaks, you know that." Sam was happy that Shaw was there. She had no one else to turn to. She couldn't tell anyone about her mother suddenly returning after thirteen years. They had agreed last night that together they would go and see Sam's father, Clint, sometime today. Mother and daughter were both unsure as to how he was going to take it, that his wife who had been gone for thirteen years was suddenly back. Together they would decide on how to release the information to the authorities.

"Where is Laura now?" Shaw asked.

"Sleeping at my place." The words sounded so strange after Sam had said them. Who would have thought she would say such a thing, that her mother was sleeping peacefully in her bed, in her cabin in the woods, with Ghost keeping guard at the foot of the bed. It sounded—and was—unbelievable.

Sam leaned into Shaw, and he put his arm around her. "You'll be fine. You've come this far when others would have given up long ago."

"But I didn't find her," Sam said, her voice sleepy. She wanted to sleep, needed to sleep, but her head was buzzing with so many unanswered questions and possibilities. "Can I crash here for a few hours, get some rest?"

"Of course."

Ironically, Sam preferred to give her mother some space. If she went back to her own place, she would be tempted to shake her awake and ask her more questions. There was plenty of time though.

"I know it's none of my business but—" Shaw began.

Sam cut him off, placing her fingers on his lips. "Don't be stupid. You are my business. What is it you want to say?"

"When you're ready, my advice to you is that the first person you should talk to, tell your story to, is Dan Miller."

Sam nodded. Over the past few weeks she had spoken to him plenty as well as local and state police. However, under Miller's lead, the FBI had taken over the Beckman case completely. Breaking the news to him about her mother made sense. It was all related to the ongoing investigation that he was in charge of.

Sam had refused to talk to reporters who had descended on the town. Thankfully, they didn't know where she lived, and they were too busy interviewing locals about Roy and Floyd Beckman. Dan Miller was the only person whom she felt comfortable with. He had a genuine concern for her well-being and wasn't pushy.

"Let him coordinate everything, press conferences and the like. He'll even run interference for you. You, your mother, and your father are going to need someone to act as a buffer between you all and the press once this is out."

Sam nuzzled a little deeper into Shaw, feeling safe and at home. "What about you?" she asked.

"What about me?"

Sam looked up into Shaw's eyes. She knew at some point he would leave, hit the road, and keep traveling, like he had told her before, leave the town behind. She had come to accept it even though she knew when that day came it would leave a huge void inside her. She didn't want him to go, but she knew he had to. Staying in one place for any length of time wasn't his style. "Stay." Sam reached up and kissed him long, deep, and hard. "I want you to stay," she said, her voice husky, her cheeks flushed in anticipation. Sam reached down to his belt, all thoughts of sleep and rest suddenly pushed aside.

---

He left town the same way he had arrived.

The sky was dark and clear, with the barest smudge of stars. The moon, with its blotched and pockmarked surface, shone big and luminescent white.

He wanted no fanfare, no send-off, despite Sam's insistence that she drive him the sixty miles to Concord, the capital of New Hampshire. As a compromise, he agreed for her to drop him at the bottom of the mountain range so he could catch a ride on the interstate.

It was quiet this time of night, just a few cars. Shaw hitched up his small backpack and raised the collar of his leather jacket as he walked along the shoulder of the highway.

A few minutes later, he heard the distinct sound of a truck behind him, its gears downshifting as it began to slow, the broad beam of its headlights cutting across the lane before illuminating the ground in front of Shaw.

Shaw turned, brought his hand up to shield his eyes from the glare.

The dark mass of a truck loomed toward him, bright orange side lights dotted its outline, and the driver perched behind the wheel in the cabin. The truck slowed, brakes hissed, and it finally came to a stop twenty yards in front of Shaw on the highway shoulder.

Reaching the truck, Shaw climbed the side step and glanced inside the cabin at the driver. An honest face and a warm smile greeted him.

The man was old. Maybe in his mid-sixties, with gray hair fashioned into a ponytail and matching beard. He had intelligent, bright eyes, the kind of eyes that had witnessed a lot.

The last twelve months on the road had made the truck driver more cynical, more cautious, more selective. Yet his ambition and enthusiasm had never burned brighter as it did right now, fueled by something most folks would never understand. He was heavyset with powerful shoulders, thick, deeply tanned forearms, and large rough hands that gripped the wheel.

"Where you heading?"

"South," Shaw replied.

The old man gave a nod to the passenger seat next to him. "Hop in, then."

Shaw swung open the door and climbed in.

"What's your name, traveler?"

Shaw settled into the truck seat, placed his backpack in the foot well between his legs. "Ben."

The old man offered his hand to Shaw. "I'm Sam. Pleased to meet you, Ben."

Ben smiled. He'd just said goodbye to one Sam, only to be greeted by another—albeit a completely different Sam. He took Sam's hand. It was huge, meaty, like a bear's paw. Shaw thought back to the words he had said to Samantha: "It's funny how the world works at times."

241

Sam reached down, pulled out a bottle, and held it toward Shaw. "Here, have a drink, Ben. I can't because I'm driving. But you go right ahead."

Ben looked at the bottle of bourbon in Sam's outreached hand.

Sam gave the bottle a tempting wiggle. "It will make the journey a lot easier for you. Might even get some sleep."

Shaw took the bottle, unscrewed the cap, and held it to his lips. "Cheers."

Sam returned the toast with a salute of his hand. "Here's to you, Ben, and wherever the open road takes you next."

Shaw took a swig from the bottle.

The engine revved, gears locked into place, brakes released, and the truck lurched forward, gathering speed as it angled back onto the highway.

Sam selected the track from the CD player in the dash and gave a discerning nod at Shaw.

Shaw settled into the comfortable seat and gazed out into the darkness, letting the warmth of the bourbon soothe his insides. Moments later he could feel his eyelids grow heavy. He let himself succumb to the hypnotic throb of the engine and gentle pulse of the passing highway lights. He jerked awake a few times, but finally he gave up the fight and closed his eyes.

As a track on the CD began to play, the bottle of bourbon was gently eased from Shaw's fingers, and the cap expertly screwed back on with one hand.

Then the haunting voice of Jim Morrison filled the cabin.

*"Riders on the storm ... "*

## THE END.

# If You Enjoyed This Book

Thank you for investing your time and money in me. I hope you enjoyed my book and it allowed you to escape from your world for a few minutes, for a few hours or even for a few days.

I would really appreciate it if you could post an honest review on any of the publishing platforms that you use. It would mean a lot to me personally, as I read every review that I get and you would be helping me become a better author. By posting a review, it will also allow other readers to discover me, and the worlds that I build. Hopefully they too can escape from their reality for just a few moments each day.

For news about me, new books and exclusive material then please:

- Follow me on Facebook: JK Ellem on Facebook
- Follow me on Instagram: @ellemjk
- Follow me on Goodreads
- Follow me on Bookbub
- Visit my Website: www.jkellem.com

# About The Author

JK Ellem was born in London and spent his formative years preferring to read books and comics rather than doing his homework.

He is the innovative author of cutting-edge popular adult thriller fiction. He likes writing thrillers that are unpredictable, have multiple layers and sub-plots that tend to lead his readers down the wrong path with twists and turns that they cannot see coming. He writes in the genres of crime, mystery, suspense and psychological thrillers.

JK is obsessed with improving his craft and loves honest feedback from his fans. His idea of success is to be stopped in the street by a supermodel in a remote European village where no one speaks English and asked to autograph one of his books and to take a quick selfie.

He has a fantastic dry sense of humor that tends to get him into trouble a lot with his wife and three children.

He splits his time between the US, the UK and Australia.

Made in the USA
Middletown, DE
09 August 2021